"How could she have done this to me?"

Max shouted.

The lawyer spread his hands. "It was an honest mistake. The laws change so often, Max."

Max whirled around, his eyes narrowed. "Don't try to cover up for her. Everyone defends her. Such a sweet girl, such a lady. *Hah!* They don't really know her. I do. She did this just to drive me crazy." He glared across the desk. "You're sure about this. *Completely* sure?"

The lawyer nodded. The Sutherland-Rafferty divorce wasn't worth the paper it had been written on. Maximillian Rafferty was still very much a married man.

Then Max smiled—a slow, lazy, dangerous smile. "So it's true. The lovely Ms. Sutherland and I are still married. Well, I'll be damned."

D0187620

Dear Reader,

Aahh . . . the lazy days of August. Relax in your favorite lawn chair with a glass of ice-cold lemonade and the perfect summertime reading . . . Silhouette Romance novels.

Silhouette Romance books *always* reflect the magic of love in compelling stories that will make you laugh and cry and move you time and time again. This month is no exception. Our heroines find happiness with the heroes of their dreams—from the boy next door to the handsome, mysterious stranger. We guarantee their heartwarming stories of love will delight you.

August continues our WRITTEN IN THE STARS series. Each month in 1991, we're proud to present a book that focuses on the hero—and his astrological sign. This month, we feature the proud, charismatic and utterly charming Leo man in Kasey Michaels's *Lion on the Prowl*.

In the months to come, watch for Silhouette Romance books by your all-time favorites, including Diana Palmer, Brittany Young and Annette Broadrick. We're pleased to bring you books with Silhouette's distinctive blend of charm, wit and—above all—romance. Your response to these stories is a touchstone for us. We'd love to hear from you!

Sincerely,

Valerie Susan Hayward
Senior Editor

KASEY MICHAELS

Lion on the Prowl

Published by Silhouette Books New York

America's Publisher of Contemporary Romance

To Tara Gavin,
who was kind enough to trust me with this project;
and to my own lovable, loyal, generous,
gorgeous, maddening Leo—my husband, Mike.

SILHOUETTE BOOKS
300 E. 42nd St., New York, N.Y. 10017

LION ON THE PROWL

Copyright © 1991 by Kasey Michaels

MORE ABOUT THE LEO MAN
Copyright © 1991 by Harlequin Enterprises B.V.

The publisher acknowledges Lydia Lee's contribution to
the afterword contained in this book.

All rights reserved. Except for use in any review,
the reproduction or utilization of this work in
whole or in part in any form by any electronic,
mechanical or other means, now known or
hereafter invented, including xerography,
photocopying and recording, or in any information
storage or retrieval system, is forbidden without
the permission of the publisher, Silhouette Books,
300 E. 42nd St., New York, N.Y. 10017

ISBN: 0-373-08808-6

First Silhouette Books printing August 1991

All the characters in this book have no existence
outside the imagination of the author and have
no relation whatsoever to anyone bearing the same
name or names. They are not even distantly
inspired by any individual known or unknown
to the author, and all incidents are pure invention.

®: Trademark used under license and
registered in the United States Patent and
Trademark Office and in other countries.

Printed in the U.S.A.

Books by Kasey Michaels

Silhouette Romance

Maggie's Miscellany #331
Compliments of the Groom #542
Popcorn and Kisses #572
To Marry at Christmas #616
His Chariot Awaits #701
Romeo in the Rain #743
Lion on the Prowl #808

KASEY MICHAELS,

the author of more than two dozen books, divides her creative time between Silhouette Romance and Regency novels. Married and the mother of four, Kasey's writing has garnered the RWA Golden Medallion Award and the *Romantic Times* Best Regency Trophy.

A Note From The Author:

Dear Reader,

When my editor, Tara Gavin, phoned to invite me to write for WRITTEN IN THE STARS, I was thrilled. But when she said my "assignment" would be Leo, I laughed out loud. Married for twenty-eight years to Mike, a classic Leo, I consider myself an expert on the male quirks of the sign! Whenever Max, my hero, was faced with a situation, I merely had to close my eyes and think, "What would Mike do?"

Yes, a Leo can be quite a handful. He will change the television station without asking because, obviously, you will want to watch what he wants to watch. He will overtip, dream wild, extravagant dreams, indulge in fierce temper tantrums and sulk when he thinks he has been injured. But he will also be loyal, loving, dependable and—thank goodness!—never afraid to say, "I love you." With a Leo there will always be a tug of wills, but the "fringe benefits" are the best in the world!

Sincerely,

Kasey Michaels

Prologue

O! the blood more stirs
To rouse a lion than to start a hare!
— William Shakespeare, *Henry IV*

The minute Maximillian Rafferty walked into a room, everyone gathered there either loved him or hated him. Most people loved Max, or at least were drawn to his vibrant good looks, lazy smile, confident stride and open, friendly manner.

Those few whose hackles rose at their first sight of him thought Max an overblown, overpowering, swaggering egomaniac, and they would ask nothing more of life than the opportunity to punch him one squarely in his perfect white teeth.

It had always been that way with Max. There existed no middle ground. People either adored him or loathed him, but no one ever admitted to being indifferent to him—and no one could ignore his presence.

It may have been his king-of-the-jungle walk that annoyed some people, the smooth, catlike grace with which Max propelled his tall, leanly muscled body through a crowd as if he expected it to part for him—which, of course, it always did.

It could have had something to do with his powerful good looks, his full head of barely tamed tawny hair, his healthy complexion, his sparkling blue eyes or even his finely chiseled chin. Or perhaps it was his voice that held the answer—that deep velvet purr that whispered the promise of hidden sensuality to women while reminding men that when a sleek jungle cat isn't purring, it growls.

As for Max, he never noticed his few detractors. He was always too busy greeting old friends or making new ones. Max loved people, and his contented purr proved it. Within five minutes of entering a party Max may have thrilled a proud father by remembering the names of all his offspring, suggested a new grip to a golfer struggling to cure a wicked slice, told a quick joke to a group of bored men propping up the bar, complimented an elderly woman on her new hairstyle, heartily greeted a businessman whose company he had saved by way of a no-interest personal loan that hadn't yet been repaid, and somehow, with minimal effort on his part, made the room and everyone in it his own.

Max's business associates had heard his roar many times, however, for his temper ran quick and white-hot when things didn't go the way he believed they should. First he'd bellow, and then he'd shut himself away and sulk. But he returned to the fray before too long, for Max loved company.

His temper cooled just as swiftly, if everyone stayed out of his way, and the return of his usual good humor would be heralded by a boyish grin and a change of subject.

He never apologized for being wrong, for Max couldn't possibly be at fault. Circumstances, bad luck, or someone else's errors were Max's explanation for problems, business or personal. But not Max. No, never Max.

When angered, he saw himself as the innocent victim of a cruel world, a man without an evil bone in his entire body. The sheer power of Max's personality had people who knew themselves to be in the right apologizing to *him*—and meaning it.

His mind had already been proven sharp and incisive, his will to succeed second nature since he'd learned to walk at the age of nine months. Max had graduated from Lehigh University in three years, bought his first company at the age of twenty-four and had owned half a dozen more two years before his thirtieth birthday.

Majestic Enterprises had become a model of the ideal conglomerate, and Max was honored by his peers, loved by his employees and respected by his critics—but he could not be duplicated. Majestic Enterprises was Max, and Max was Majestic Enterprises.

Max liked to paint with a broad brush, making sweeping strokes on the canvas of life, and left the details to his trusted employees who ran along behind him, figuratively sweeping up the boring paperwork. He worked best that way, seeing the whole picture, his unflagging optimism blending perfectly with his daring, intelligent and instinctive business sense. He worked hard and he played hard and, in general, Max was a happy man.

But even the optimistic Max recognized the fact that no one lives forever, although he certainly didn't dwell on the idea. Much as he disliked paperwork, at thirty-two he acknowledged that the time had come to draft a will.

After closing the deal on Blair Manufacturing, bringing the number of businesses under his conglomerate umbrella to fourteen, Max emptied a dresser drawer stuffed full with his personal papers and dumped them in his lawyer's lap with the vague order that Paul Bridgeman should "do something with this mess."

A week later the plate glass windows of Bridgeman's sixth-floor corner office rattled from the mighty blast of Max Rafferty's injured roar.

Chapter One

The lion was roaring—again. Sitting at ease one moment, his long, graceful body flattering the leather chair he sat in, Max Rafferty had sprung to his feet, prowling his lawyer's Oriental carpet and angrily growling his displeasure almost before Paul Bridgeman had stopped speaking.

Paul cringed behind his desk, not daring to move, and hoped for invisibility.

"You're wrong, Paul. You must be wrong. I don't believe it! How could she have done this to me? My, God, Paul—can't the woman even *count?*"

The lawyer spread his hands, shrugging. "It was an honest mistake. The laws change so often, Max. What's considered legal one day is changed the next. You've done business in those South American countries. You know what it's like."

Max whirled around to glare at Paul, his eyes narrowed menacingly. "Don't try to cover up for her. My God, you haven't even met her and you're defending her. Everyone defends her." The clear blue eyes compressed another fraction. "'Such a sweet girl,' they say, 'such a lady.' *Hah!* But they don't really know her. I do. Lord, do I know her! She did this on purpose, just to drive me crazy."

The lawyer frowned. "Why would she want to do that?"

"Why else? Because she *hates* me!" Max snarled, baring his even white teeth. He resumed his pacing, his head unbowed, eyeing the lawyer dangerously, reminding Paul of a lithe, fearsome caged beast crossing and recrossing the length of its cage, planning its escape. Or its revenge.

"I—I think you're wrong, Max," Paul offered weakly. "I mean, she sent this copy to you two years ago. If it was a ploy, if she didn't believe it was legal, wouldn't she have contacted you again by now? Perhaps she's as in the dark about this mess as you were."

Max snatched up the wrinkled paper, the one he himself had stuffed into his dresser drawer two years earlier, and walked to the large window overlooking the downtown Manhattan street to examine the document for the first time. When he had received it two years ago he had recognized it for what it was, crushed it into a ball and flung it at the nearest wall. At the time, the last thing he wanted was to read the fine print.

After a long, uncomfortable silence Max retraced his steps to fling the paper on the desktop. "I can't make head or tail of this thing. It looks legal enough, with all those seals and ribbons." He leaned his palms on the glass-topped surface as he glared across the desk at the lawyer. "You're sure about this? *Completely* sure?"

Paul Bridgeman nodded his head, wincing. The Sutherland-Rafferty divorce, obtained in an obscure South American country, wasn't worth the crumpled, beribboned paper it had been written on. Maximillian Rafferty, mastermind behind the sprawling Majestic Enterprises, and supposed eligible bachelor, was still very much a married man.

Just as Paul began mentally reviewing his life insurance portfolio, Max smiled, a slow, lazy smile that the lawyer tentatively returned. It appeared that the worst was over—for the lawyer.

"So it's true. The lovely Ms. Sutherland and I are still married," Max mused slowly, his now-quiet voice low, reflective. "Well, I'll be damned."

Julia Sutherland stood very still—a cool, serene oasis in the center of an ever-growing storm. Not a single strand of her long, burnt-cinnamon hair was out of place as it hung gracefully to precisely three inches below her shoulders, then curved smoothly under in a sleek pageboy style.

The perfect oval of her face and finely drawn features resembled warm, touchable ivory, so that her subtle, expertly applied makeup defied detection as it lent definition to her sensuously full mouth and added an air of mystery to her midnight-dark eyes.

Her pale, whisper-green silk blouse and slacks bore the classic Sutherland trademark of impeccable styling: the pleated cossack blouse flowing smoothly as it tucked inside a wide fabric belt, the matching slacks molded closely to her slim hips only to widen gracefully as they fell to her shoe tops. Sutherland clothing was designed to be flattering, and they flattered no one better than their designer, Julia Sutherland.

The only sign of agitation could be seen in an involuntary movement of her right hand as she raised it to briefly touch the waist-length double strand of pearls that hung around her slim neck. But the hand was almost immediately brought down to her side as Julia took a single steadying breath and surveyed the overcrowded dressing room, blocking out the near hysteria of models and dressers as she sought the answer to this latest problem.

It took her only a moment to come to a decision. Walking over to a table piled high with odd bolts of fabric, pins, buttons and other accessories, she picked up scissors and cut a generous length of dark paisley silk from one bolt.

"Come here, Marilou," she ordered quietly, and the model, who had been frantically searching for the belt to the outfit she was to wear down the runway in precisely thirty seconds, raced to Julia's side.

"Raise your arms, dear," Julia said, unclasping her pearls and twirling them lengthwise around the swath of material. She deftly tied the pearl-wrapped material loosely around Marilou's waist, tucking in the raw ends and securing them discreetly with a large safety pin before adjusting the improvised belt so that it rode low on the model's left hip.

"It's perfect!" the model exclaimed, obviously impressed with the result. "I like this even better than the belt you designed for it. You've done it again, Ms. Sutherland."

"Thank you, Marilou," Julia answered sincerely, turning the willow-thin girl around for one last inspection of the simply cut midnight-blue evening gown, approving of the way the new belt complemented the chandelier-size pearl earrings Marilou wore. "You're up next—do me proud!"

Six hours later, after taking the runway herself to accept the cheers and applause of the appreciative audience of department and specialty store buyers and several members of the press, Julia and her assistant, Holly Hollis, were in the rear seat of a rented limousine, on their way out of Manhattan and headed back to Allentown.

While Julia relaxed, her long, straight legs stretched out so that her silk-stockinged feet rested on the jump seat facing her, her head leaning back against the plush burgundy cushions, her assistant was busily going through the thick sheaf of papers that lay on her lap.

"We've got enough orders here to keep everyone busy for several months," Holly told her boss delightedly. "I knew your fall designs were good, Julia, but I never expected this, even when I read your horoscope in the newspaper this morning and it predicted that today would prove to be a red-letter day— a real eyepopper, I think it said."

"If only I had known that earlier, Holly," Julia responded dryly, her fists pushed deep in the slash pockets of her slacks, for she had given up smoking three months earlier and was still finding it difficult to think of something to do with her hands. "Just imagine all the worry such reliable information could have saved me—not to mention the work. I should have consulted you sooner, had you read my tea leaves for me or something. Why, you might even have been able to tell me to be prepared with a substitute belt for the blue velvet."

Holly wrinkled her small, turned-up nose. "Smart aleck," she groused good-naturedly. "You don't fool me, Julia. You're a Scorpion, and everybody knows that Scorpions are intrigued by the occult," Holly continued, waggling her fingers in front of Julia's face, "and by *all* things mysterious and unexplained. The only reason you're pretending not to be is because you're afraid you'll get too involved, which is another thing Scorpions do."

Julia turned her head to look at her assistant, who was also her good friend. "Right," she said genially. "If the truth were told, I have a closet full of voodoo dolls at home, all wearing Sutherland originals, of course."

"Astrology has nothing to do with voodoo dolls. And it's the truth, Julia. Think about smoking. You smoked like a chimney for almost five years, then quit in a day. That's always the way it is with you Scorpions, all or nothing. And don't think it's so dark in this limo that I can't see you making faces at me—oh, forget it, you're a hopeless case. Look," Holly said, pointing toward a red glowing dome visible through the wide window. "There's the light on top of the Pennsylvania Power and Light Company. We're almost home."

Holly began gathering up the order forms, stuffing them in the attaché case that lay on the floor, while Julia sat up straight, adjusting her pearls and reaching for her ivory mohair cape.

"I'm dead on my feet, Holly," Julia told her friend, dragging one hand through the top of her hair, its blunt-cut length rearranging itself perfectly around her face. "Do you mind that I told the driver to drop me first?"

Her assistant shook her head. "You're the boss, remember? Besides, I think I might have the driver deposit me at my mother's. She'll love it if the neighbors see me driving up in a long white limo. As a matter of fact, the only thing she'd like better would be if I stepped out of it in a bridal gown, trailing my rich, adoring groom behind me."

Julia grinned wryly. "A man? Does your mother honestly believe a man is the answer to every woman's dreams? Buy a dog, Holly. Take it from me, they're less trouble."

Holly maneuvered her size-five body into a full-length camel hair coat as the limousine turned onto Hamilton Street. "Oh, sure, Julia, that's easy for you to say. You've got Luke."

"You make it sound like I roped and tied him," Julia said, looking down at the exquisite marquise-cut diamond ring circling the third finger of her left hand.

"And this ring is a token of love, Holly, not a brand of possession."

"Call it what you want, Julia, I still want one. I want all of it—the man, the ring, the three-bedroom house in the suburbs, the two-point-whatever kids, even the dirty laundry. And you have to admit it, Luke Manning is a wonderful man."

Julia sighed wistfully. "I know, Holly, I know. I just wish—hey, looks like this is my stop." She took the attaché case from her friend's outstretched hand. "Don't bother calling me tomorrow, Holly. I plan to stay in bed all day, recovering. And, listen, since it's Saturday night, why don't you skip your mother's and have the driver take you to Charley's Pub for their weekly singles bash? My treat. Maybe you'll find your Prince Charming waiting there, glass slipper in hand, and the two of you can use the limo to drive off into the sunset—or sunrise."

Holly grinned wickedly and leaned forward to tap on the pane of smoked glass dividing the passenger compartment from the driver's seat. "You've got a deal, boss. See you Monday."

Julia stepped out onto the wide sidewalk, lifting her head to gaze up at the clear, star-dotted night sky. It was just past seven o'clock and she had been up since an hour before dawn. She smiled at the stars twinkling down on her, feeling a rush of satisfaction as she then directed her gaze toward the large Victorian house she had purchased a year earlier.

The house was visible proof of her hard work, and she loved each piece of original oak woodwork and every stained glass topped window of its three spacious floors. An anachronism in this age of cookie-cutter condos and bland modern architecture, the house held just the sort of solid respectability and livable hominess Julia craved, even if she and her dog, Wellington, rattled around in its twelve rooms that could have easily housed three generations of Sutherlands.

Julia walked up the three cement steps that gave access to a wide, grass-edged walkway and another, broader set of six wooden steps ending on the porch, which glowed softly in the overhead light that was controlled by a timer connected to her security system.

She fumbled in her slim leather shoulder bag for her keys, grumbling under her breath as her fingers closed over her wallet, a comb, two lipsticks—everything but the elusive key chain.

"Damn," she swore softly, preparing to dump the contents of the purse on top of the painted rattan table that stood to the right of the door.

"Tut, tut, Julia, mustn't swear. It's not good for the image" warned a deep male voice from the area of the porch where a small grouping of matching rattan chairs sat cloaked in darkness.

Julia's movements stilled. She unhurriedly lifted her head, her crown of burnt-cinnamon hair gleaming warmly in the porch light as she stared unblinkingly into the darkness.

"Hello, Max," she said matter-of-factly, just as if his reappearance in her life hadn't shocked her right down to her toes.

* * *

Max believed himself prepared for his initial meeting with Julia Sutherland Rafferty, for his first good look at the woman who had walked into his life unexpectedly five years earlier and, within the matter of a heartbeat, turned that life upside down.

He felt confident that he was over her, that he was immune to her cool, elegant beauty and the exquisitely formed, long-legged body that she carried with the grace of a queen.

Her midnight eyes, he was sure, no longer held the key to his soul. The low, faintly husky sound of her voice no longer drew him like a siren song.

He was free of her. Free of Julia Sutherland, who was still—God help them both—Mrs. Maximillian Rafferty.

He had driven down from Manhattan that afternoon to confront her with his startling discovery, just so he could watch her squirm. It was going to be poetic justice.

As he drove along the interstate highway that had been constructed since his last visit to the city, he remembered, in devastating detail, the last time he had seen her. Their last night together.

It had started well, with every indication of getting better by the minute. Julia had met him at the door of their uptown penthouse apartment with a melting kiss and a glass of chilled champagne, then led him into the dining room to see that she had set the table with their best china.

They had argued that morning, which was nothing new. They argued nearly every morning, just as they made extremely satisfying love every night.

After five months of marriage it seemed as if the only time they weren't at each other's throats was when they were in each other's arms, but that was something they would work out together, eventually. They had eloped after knowing each other less than three weeks, and it would take time to smooth the rough edges off their marriage.

But it had looked as if Julia had forgiven him this time—not that he had been wrong, and not that he could even remember the cause of their argument—and she was offering to bury the hatchet over an intimate candlelight dinner.

Already looking forward to the conclusion of the meal and a swift adjournment to their bedroom, Max had allowed himself to be lulled into a receptive mood, only to have Julia drop her latest bombshell.

She wanted to leave the company she had been working for and set out on her own, designing women's clothing. Not only that, but she didn't want any help from him. Not his advice. Not his money. And definitely not his opposition.

"I'm going to call it Sutherland," she had announced, reminding him for the millionth time that she refused to use his name professionally, as if the name Rafferty was chopped liver, for crying out loud. "Nothing fancy, nothing cute. Just Sutherland. What do you think?"

What had he thought? He had thought it stank, that's what he had thought, and that's what he had told her, at great length and in no uncertain terms. Throwing down his napkin, he had risen to begin pacing, roaring his disapproval while Julia, sitting serenely at the other end of the table, had said nothing.

"Are you quite finished?" she had asked when, exhausted, Max had retaken his seat, flinging himself into the chair with his usual dramatic flair. "Good. Very good."

The next few minutes still remained hazy in Max's mind, but the next thing he had known he wasn't eating linguine with clam sauce, he was *wearing* it—and Julia was gone!

Was he "over" Julia Sutherland Rafferty? He damn well was. In spades.

"What can I do for you, Max?" Julia said now, her beautiful face expressionless, any reaction to his reappearance in her life her secret, and one he instinctively knew she'd rather burn in hell for than share with him.

Max looked into Julia's eyes, those deep, dark, bottomless pools and, with sudden insight, realized that those eyes had haunted him day and night for five long years. He silently cursed himself for a fool.

He was "over" Julia?

Sure, he was.

And Napoleon had won at Waterloo.

Lord, but Max was a gorgeous animal. Just as gorgeous as he had been the day he'd walked into the classroom at Lehigh University over five years ago to give the first of three daylong seminars on entrepreneurship at his alma mater.

Julia fought the urge to throw herself into his arms, so great was her physical response to his unexpected presence on her front porch, but she caught herself in time, remembering that his overpowering physical attraction had been what had gotten her into trouble in the first place.

Having arrived, heart intact, to the mature age of twenty-six, Julia hadn't believed in love at first sight, the sort of mindless attraction that had a lot to do with hormones and very little to do with common sense. Yet Max Rafferty's appearance had blown all her theories out of the water the moment he'd turned to face the class and, scanning the roomful of eager faces, smiled directly into hers.

She hadn't smiled back at him, she remembered, and had been secretly delighted to see that this reaction, or nonreaction, had piqued his interest. Sure that he was accustomed to women falling all over him, she determined that she was not going to be his local conquest for the short time he'd be in town. No, if Max Rafferty wanted her, it would have to be for a lifetime.

Julia had followed him constantly with her eyes as she silently willed him to look in her direction again and recognize, as she had, that they belonged together.

When the class ended she had lingered a moment, writing the last points of his speech in her notebook, giving him time to approach her if he wanted to do so. She still didn't know why she had felt so confident that he would come, but she hadn't been surprised when a shadow fell over her desk and she looked up into the clear Siberian-husky blue of his lively eyes.

She had remained in control as they walked together across the historic campus to grab a cup of coffee at the student center. Her mind still ruled her heart when she had accepted his dinner invitation. Reason had won out over inclination as she had dressed in one of her own designs and accompanied him to the intimate, candle lit restaurant.

It had been the innocent touch of his hand that destroyed her as they had both reached for the same warmed roll, their carelessly colliding fingertips sparking a raging bonfire of love and desire in the pit of her stomach that all the emotional pain and clearheaded reasoning of five long years without him hadn't successfully quenched.

They had married in haste, and had repented almost as quickly, and if their marriage hadn't ended they would have eventually killed each other, figuratively if not literally.

They had been incompatible, she and Max, incompatible everywhere that it mattered, except in bed. But, oh, how she had loved Maximillian Rafferty—how she had adored him. She would have gladly died for him, if he had asked, but she'd be damned if she'd allow herself to be buried alive by the overwhelming power of his personality.

That's what was so wonderful about Luke. Luke didn't expect her to live only for him, only through him. She wasn't a reflection of Luke, she was her own person, with her own life.

Luke. Julia fought the urge to touch the ring that Luke had slipped on her finger only a week ago. Had word of their engagement reached Max's ears in New York? Had he come to Allentown to interfere with her plans to remarry?

Julia shook her head, dismissing the thought. Max wouldn't do that. He was a lot of things, but Max was never mean. He would never deliberately hurt anyone, not even her.

She watched now as he rose from the chair, the soft whisper of his full-length leather coat reminding her of his love for creature comforts. He slowly walked into the circle of light.

"Aren't you going to invite me in?" she heard him ask as she ran her gaze over his face, registering the slight changes five years had made in him, all of them good. It was just like Max to grow more handsome with each passing year.

Invite him in? She'd rather play hostess to a family of rattlesnakes. It would be less dangerous. "Of course you may come in, Max," she answered quickly, reaching into her purse, her fingers immediately closing around the key chain that had eluded her earlier. "I'm never rude to ex-husbands."

He waited until she'd opened the front door and the two of them had stepped inside the ceramic-tiled foyer before saying in a tone she recognized instantly as his cat-who's-caught-the-canary purr, "Ex-husbands, yes, Mrs. Rafferty. But I was asking about *me*."

Chapter Two

"And what is that oblique yet snide statement supposed to mean, Max?" she asked tiredly, moving forward out of the foyer as she slipped off her cape. "You never were any good when you were trying to be cryptic. You're much more effective when you stick to your usual steamroller approach. Coffee?"

Julia raised a hand to flip on the wall switch that controlled three separate table lamps, bringing the high-ceilinged living room to life. The large navy Oriental rug, ice-blue walls and white-on-white striped satin traditional furniture piled with pastel throw pillows all bore the unwritten signature of her subdued, refined taste. The only thing that looked even marginally out of place was the presence of one very large black dog—obviously *not* a watchdog—sleeping soundly in front of the cold fireplace.

Max took in the furnishings with one assessing movement of his eyes, seeing the room for what it was, a perfect reflection of Julia's well-developed nesting instinct. The room welcomed occupants without intimidating them, its contents all balancing each other without looking stiff or regimented.

He took a seat in one corner of the comfortable couch, relaxing his tall frame against the half dozen pillows that contoured themselves against his back. "Only if it's not too much bother," he said at last, referring to Julia's offer of coffee.

She tossed the cape on a nearby chair. "It's instant, Max. I'm not about to grind the beans for you. And don't get too comfortable. You're not going to be here that long."

Max put his hands behind his head, leaned back and crossed his feet at the ankles as he deposited them on the glass-topped coffee table. "Wanna bet?"

That was his second cryptic comment in less than two minutes. Julia stopped on her way through the dining room to the kitchen to turn and look at Max carefully. He already had, in his own inimitable way, taken possession of her living room and made it his own. She hated his arrogant self-possession, even as she admired him for it.

It wasn't that Julia was unsure of herself, of her abilities, her talents, her intelligence, or her own intrinsic worth. She knew she was a capable human being. It was just that she never felt she successfully showed the world that confidence, the sort of self-assurance that effortlessly oozed from Max's every pore. He expected things to go his way, and they usually did. He expected people to like him, and they almost always complied.

If only Max's charisma, that had attracted her the first moment they'd met, had rubbed off on her, but it hadn't. Maybe that was one of the reasons their marriage had failed. Maybe she had traded in her admiration of Max for envy.

She drew herself up straight and proceeded into the kitchen, making coffee with swift, efficient movements. This wasn't the time for reflection, for dragging out long-ago pain for yet another examination. Max had something up his sleeve, the rat, or he wouldn't be here in her living room. And she'd rather eat dirt than ask him what it was.

By the time she returned to the living room, carrying two steaming cups of instant coffee on a small silver tray, Wellington—the traitor—was lying on the white couch, his head in Max's lap.

"Wellington," Julia warned quietly, believing she had won the battle to keep the large black dog off the white couch months ago. "What do you think you're doing?"

The dog, who had won Julia's heart with his enormous brown eyes the day she'd seen him at the pound—having gone there to find a small dog, only to come home with a seventy-pound canine shedding machine of dubious lineage—rolled onto his back so that Max would scratch his hairy stomach.

"Wellington, huh?" Max commented, taking the cup from the tray Julia offered. "You always were fascinated with the Napoleonic Wars, weren't you, hon?"

The casually inserted endearment rocked Julia to her toes, and she had to fight to hold back a sharp order for him to *never* use it again. Instead she placed the tray on the coffee table and picked up her own cup. "I was crazy about their uniforms," she lied neatly, concentrating on not spilling a drop of the hot liquid, thus betraying herself even more. "The gowns of the era were interesting, too, with their sheer, pale fabrics and high-waisted, childlike look that the ladies circumvented nicely by dampening the material so that it clung to their bodies."

His blue eyes twinkled. "Sounds like a fashion trend I'd like to see come back for an encore," Max quipped, putting down his cup. "If nothing else, you seem to have used the light colors. What do you call the one you're wearing—*barely* green? All right, Wellington," he said, snapping his fingers as he sat forward, lifting his feet from the coffee table just as Julia was contemplating removing them less subtly—most probably at the knees, with a dull-edged kitchen knife. "Time to get down."

Wellington complied immediately, hopping to the floor to curl up at Max's feet, and issued a deep, contented doggy sigh before lapsing once more into a stupor.

"Rotten mutt," Julia grumbled, glaring at the animal. "You always were good at collecting adoring subjects, weren't you, Max?"

"You know what they say, Julia, you can't fool kids or dogs. Besides, it didn't take me long to *collect* you, as I recall," he answered easily, stunning her with one of his sunny smiles. "Not that the attraction wasn't mutual."

"When it comes to ancient history, Max, I'd much rather discuss the Napoleonic Wars, thank you," Julia answered quickly, knowing that Max hadn't so much "collected" her as complied with her intense unspoken desire to have him—not that she had ever informed Max of that particular fact. What was that saying Holly used so often? Oh, yes. *He chased her until she caught him.* Julia fought the urge to wince at the truth of the saying, and stiffened her spine.

"Now, charmed as I am that you've deigned to come all the way to Allentown to see me—considering the fact that such a distance has hitherto seemed unbreachable—I'd appreciate it if you'd come to the point."

"The point? And you're dragging out all your best English, too, just like you used to do when you wanted people to believe you were actually civilized. But I remember the broken china, and the slammed doors—and the rest of it. What's the matter, hon? You didn't used to be so slow on the uptake. Haven't you figured it out yet?"

"Oh, put a muzzle on it, Max," Julia ordered automatically, mentally retracing their conversation from the moment Max had made his presence known to her on the front porch. As a rule, she enjoyed a mystery, but she was in no mood to play investigator. She just wanted Max to tell her what was on his mind and get out of her life—her hard-won, placid, uneventful life. "I don't know what you're—oh, there goes the doorbell!"

"Don't answer it," Max ordered swiftly as Julia rose to go to the door. He was just beginning to enjoy himself, and the last thing he needed was an interruption. "It's probably just some local kid selling Girl Scout cookies."

Julia ignored him. She didn't care if it was a burglar come to case the joint, any interruption seemed better than the small, niggling feeling that Max's news wasn't going to make *her* a happy camper.

She peered through the leaded glass pane of the front door to see a familiar tall form standing on the porch. "Luke!" she exclaimed involuntarily, stepping three paces back from the door without opening it. "It's Luke," she said, turning to Max, her expression carefully blank.

"He must be important, Julia. You're becoming redundant. I heard you the first time." Max had somehow crept up behind her without her knowledge. "Luke who?" he growled, his friendly blue eyes turning alarmingly glacial.

Julia smiled as she recognized his expression as the one she had seen during their marriage whenever another man looked at her admiringly. It was just like Max to be jealous, even now.

"Luke Manning," Julia answered automatically before sensing that it was her turn to be cryptic. She smiled evilly, intending to enjoy the moment to the hilt. Raising her left hand, she wiggled her pink-tipped fingers slightly, so that the light from the foyer chandelier caught the sparkling facets of the marquise diamond. "This Luke. Get the point, Max. Or if you're feeling a little slow on the uptake, maybe I should draw you a diagram?''

He took her hand, examining the ring as if he had been asked to appraise it. "Nice. Luke Manning has good taste—but mine was bigger."

Julia pulled her hand away. She didn't know what bothered her most, Max's dig at the size of the diamond, his seeming acceptance of her engagement to Luke, or the electric tingle she'd felt when Max's fingers touched hers. Whatever it was that Max had, whatever magic had attracted her to him five years ago, he obviously hadn't lost it. The bell rang again. "I'll get the door," she said, praying she didn't sound desperate for escape.

"You do that," Max purred, his smile slow and satisfied as the sight of a flustered Julia seemed to satisfy something in his soul. "I'll just go back into the living room and leave you two lovebirds alone to say goodbye."

Julia's heart stopped—she was sure it did—then began to race at double time. *Goodbye?* She wasn't going to say goodbye to Luke. What was Max talking about? Why had he called her Mrs. Rafferty when he knew full well she had never used his name? Why had he skirted her remark about ex-husbands? What was he trying to—

"Oh . . . my . . . *God!*"

"What's the matter, hon?" Max questioned, his tone sympathetic, his maddening smile still in place. "You're looking a little pale. Uh-oh, Luke's given up the bell in favor of knocking. You'd better answer him before he breaks down the door."

Julia feared she might faint. The room had become very bright, she felt slightly sick to her stomach, and her head was spinning. She looked toward the front door, where Luke was visible through the glass, a worried frown on his face, then back to Max. "I—you and I are—*no,* that's impossible! It *is* impossible, Max, isn't it? Damn you, don't just stand there grinning, tell me it's impossible!"

"What's impossible, hon?" Max asked from the comfort of the couch. "I don't like to point this out, Julia, but you're making precious little sense."

Luke's voice came through the door. "Julia? Julia! Are you all right in there? Who are you talking to? Who's in there with you?"

Julia took one step toward the foyer, stopped, and fairly charged back into the living room. "You're enjoying this, aren't you, Max? Of course you are. You may play dumb better than anybody—heaven knows you've got the inside track on it—but you don't fool me for a minute."

"I don't?" Max snapped his fingers and Wellington woke from a deep sleep, hopped onto the couch and laid his head in Max's lap. "That's true, hon. I never could fool you, could I? But tell me anyway— what did I do that didn't fool you?"

Julia ran a hand through her hair. The glossy tresses rearranged themselves perfectly around her head, satisfying Max in a gut-clenching way he made no move to hide.

"Sutherland had its fall showing today, in Manhattan," she continued, pacing the length of the Oriental carpet, her pale green silk slacks flattering her long-legged strides. "Holly gave out press releases and included the fact that Luke and I just became engaged. You saw one of the articles and, naturally, decided to get some of your own back by coming here to scare me with some silliness about our divorce not being final or some such rot. I'm right, aren't I? Just admit it, Max, and be done with it."

The doorbell rang again, insistently, five times in succession.

"You'd better let him in, hon, before he calls out the marines. Oh, and by the way—who's Holly?"

Julia pressed a fist to her lips and slowly counted to ten. He was doing it to her again, just as he had always done it. He knew exactly which buttons to push to send her temper spinning out of control. But it wasn't going to work this time. Oh, no. This time she was going to beat him at his own game. "We aren't married, Max. I divorced you two years ago, and I have the papers to prove it."

"Really, Julia," Max responded, scratching Wellington behind the ears so that the dog appeared suspended on the edge of ecstasy. "Tell me, hon, do you *habla Español?*"

"Do I speak Spanish? No, and neither do you. What does that have to say to anything?"

"I didn't think you did. Pity. My lawyer speaks Spanish. He even counts in Spanish."

"Bully for your lawyer. Maybe he'll get to do a stint on *Sesame Street,*" Julia spat, willing herself to stand very still until she conquered the urge to strangle Max—and Wellington as well.

"Yes, bully for Paul. I could bore you with all the depressing details, Julia, but I can sense that you'd rather I cut to the bottom line. You didn't fulfill the residency requirements for a divorce, dear wife— missed it, in fact, by a full two days. It seems, difficult as you might find this to believe, that you and I are still married."

"*Married!*"

It was bad enough to hear the word aloud, but hearing it in stereo was overwhelming.

Julia whirled around to see Luke Manning standing behind her, his deep brown eyes narrowed menacingly. "The door was open, darling. I tried the knob when I began to think you weren't ever going to answer it," he said quietly, striding past Julia as if she didn't really exist, to place himself squarely in front of Max. "Let me take a wild guess here—you're Maximillian Rafferty."

"And you're Luke Manning," Max responded genially. "Wellington," he scolded mildly, "be a good dog and go away so that I can stand up and greet Mr. Manning properly. That's a good dog."

Rising once Wellington had grudgingly left his comfortable resting place, Max smiled and extended his right hand across the coffee table. Luke took it, willingly or unwillingly only he knew.

"Good to meet you, Luke, although the circumstances could have been better. Julia, honey, it looks like we've become a party. Do you want to call out for pizzas or do you have something in the kitchen we can offer our guest?"

It was a bad dream, Julia decided, wildly searching for an explanation to the bizarre scene unfolding in front of her eyes. She had fallen asleep in the limousine and any minute now Holly would wake her to tell her they were home. It had to be a bad dream, a terribly twisted nightmare. Nothing this bizarre ever happened in real life. Did it?

She briefly closed her eyes. No, nothing like this happened in real life—unless Max was somehow involved. She opened her eyes to see that Luke was now sitting beside Max on the couch, telling him that he had moved to Allentown three years ago to practice pediatric surgery.

She spread her hands, only to clench her fists and bring them to her mouth. She couldn't believe it. Her entire world was shattering before her eyes and the two men in her life were just sitting there, calmly making polite conversation. Was she the only sane person left in the room? Didn't they understand that she was about to explode?

"Max!" she said, a bit too loudly, in order to get his attention as he was telling Luke that one of his companies was involved in designing a new cardiac-care wing for a children's hospital in Pittsburgh.

"Excuse me, Luke," Max said, turning to Julia. "You bellowed, sweetheart?"

She forced a polite smile. "May I see you in the kitchen for a minute, Max?" she asked, consciously donning the armor of cool civility that had served her so well over the years.

Max grinned, winking at her. "Of course you may, hon. Luke, you will excuse us, won't you?"

Luke shook his head. "No, Max, I don't think I will. I have a feeling anything you and Julia have to discuss includes me as well. Am I wrong?"

Max looked at Luke, at Julia's fiancé, and recognized the intelligence in the man's all-seeing eyes. He was as dark and cool as Max knew himself to be bright and sunny, and he reminded Max of Julia more than anyone else he'd ever met. He didn't relish the idea of dealing with two people who exhibited such outward composure and dogged determination.

Luke was a handsome man, if Max was any judge, as tall as Max himself, with black hair, a deeply tanned complexion, and a well-chiseled face with enough planes and angles to support him in style if he opted to leave medicine and make his living doing magazine ads for cigarettes.

Max turned on the charm, deciding to take his best shot. "You're right, Luke, this does concern you. Please believe me when I say—" he turned his head slightly to look at Julia for a moment "—that I didn't even know of your existence when I came to Allentown today. But, be that as it may, and much as I know you're not going to like hearing it, I found out yesterday that Julia and I are still legally married."

Knowing his wife well enough to be sure she had already gotten her emotions back under control, Max concentrated on Luke's reaction to his news. The man reacted by not reacting, once again reminding Max of Julia. It didn't do a lot for his ego.

"That's easily rectified, Max," Luke put in calmly, rising to go to Julia. He slipped an arm around her slim, belted waist, and Max fumed as Julia lightly leaned against the man's long body, as if to show her husband exactly where her affections lay. "We'll just have to postpone the wedding until you two get another divorce."

Max grimaced, as if unwilling to hurt Luke. Julia was sure he held no such compunction about hurting her, for she had been hurting like hell ever since Max had said hello.

"You'd think so, Luke, wouldn't you? There's only one thing. You see, I thought my feelings for Julia had died the day I received the divorce decree, but it only took one look at her tonight to prove to me that I was mistaken. Our divorce was a terrible mistake, Luke, although maybe it was also a lucky mistake. We're both older now, wiser, and I've discovered that I still love her. Very much. No, the last thing I want is a divorce. I want us to try again."

When Max finished speaking, there was a long, strained silence before Julia turned to Luke and said firmly, "Luke—darling—go home. I'll phone you in the morning."

Luke ignored her, pushing her hands away as he took a step in Max's direction. "You want to try again? Are you crazy? She doesn't love you. She loves me. Sorry Max. You had your chance, and you blew it."

Julia winced, knowing that Luke, who could have said anything at all, had said exactly the wrong thing. It took either a very brave or a very foolish person to tell Maximillian Rafferty that he had lost. Max hated to lose, even more than Luke did—and Luke was not a cheerful loser.

Max's genial smile disappeared as the heat of battle came into his eyes. "Lost, have I? What's the matter, Manning, are you afraid of a little competition? You said she loves you. If you're right you have nothing to worry about. But I'm not going away. She's my wife and I'm going to fight for her."

"*She*," Julia interrupted hotly, placing her body between the two men, "is tired of being referred to as a pronoun! And *she* is not about to stand here and be fought over by two men who don't seem to think *her* opinion matters! I'm not a trophy, Max. Luke, as I said before—go home. I'm a big girl now, and I can handle my own problems."

The two men continued to glare at each other for a moment, then Luke bent to kiss Julia full on the mouth. "Phone me in the morning," he said, looking deeply into her eyes. "Sooner, if you have to."

Julia nodded, disliking the feeling that Luke hadn't so much kissed her as he had attempted to establish his ownership of her. Did all men think a marriage license was also a bill of sale?

"Rafferty," Luke said shortly, nodding in Max's general direction before turning for the door.

"It's been a pleasure meeting you, Luke," Max called after him, sitting down once more. Once the door had closed behind Luke, Max looked up to see Julia glaring down at him with murder in her eyes. "Nice man, Julia, although your taste in men has always been good, so I knew immediately that he wouldn't be a jerk. It's almost a shame you're going to have to break his heart. By the way, sweetheart, I know why you sent him home, and I think you were right."

"Why did I send him home?" Julia asked dully, wondering why she was even stooping to talk with the man.

Max smiled, his voice low and amused. "You sent him home, sweetheart, because poor old Luke still thinks you are the most serene, collected, together female in the entire western hemisphere, and you didn't want to blow the image. But he's gone now, so you can feel free to pick up that pretty vase over there and throw it at my head."

"I don't do that anymore," Julia answered tightly, wishing it was completely true. She hadn't thrown anything in years—not since she had crowned Max with the linguine—but the urge to do so now was nearly overpowering.

Max stood up, stretching like a big cat that had just risen from an enjoyable nap. "That's a relief, because I have some more good news for you. I'm moving in."

Julia's gaze flew to the vase on the coffee table. "The hell you are, Max Rafferty!" she exploded, biting her lips as she realized she had nearly allowed her temper to defeat her.

"The hell I am, Julia Rafferty," Max responded in a warning growl, already on his way to the front door. "My suitcase is on the front porch. And I wouldn't advise you to lock the door behind me, because I'd only break that pretty window over there to get back in. You know I would, don't you, hon?"

"I hate you," Julia gritted from between clenched teeth.

"No, you don't," Max answered, his hand on the doorknob. "And I did mean what I said earlier, Julia. Crazy as it sounds, I still love you. I love you very much—and I'm going to get you back."

"Wanna bet?" Julia challenged, using Max's own words, only he had already left the room and didn't hear her.

Chapter Three

Julia locked the bedroom door behind her, whether against Max or to protect herself from her own weakness, she didn't know, and walked to the closet, fumbling with the small pearl buttons on her blouse cuffs.

Max was still downstairs in her kitchen, finishing off the two homemade meatloaf sandwiches she had made him, surreptitiously feeding scraps to Wellington, who had camped himself under the glass-topped table as if he believed she couldn't see him breaking another Sutherland house rule.

She had put clean sheets on the king-size brass bed in the largest guest room, secretly enjoying the mental picture of the masculine Max being reduced to sleeping on pink flowered sheets, and unwrapped a fresh bar of unscented soap for the bathroom that adjoined the bedroom.

Depositing her blouse and slacks in the hamper, she rid herself of her underwear and quickly donned the years-old full-length flannel nightgown she usually reserved for those rare times she was ill and in need of homey comfort. The last thing she wanted to feel next to her skin tonight was clingy, seductive silk.

Walking into her bathroom, she tied back her hair and began creaming off her makeup, a nightly ritual she had never abandoned before and refused to skip tonight, even if it was after midnight and she was dead on her feet after living through the longest day on record—and even though she didn't want to meet her reflection in the mirror above the sink.

Julia could hear Max moving around in the room below her, the sound of rushing water telling her that he was rinsing off his dishes and would probably be upstairs in less than a minute. Her movements made clumsy by her haste, she grabbed the soap and quickly washed her face before turning off the lights and hopping into bed.

She counted silently as his footsteps climbed the fourteen stairs to the second floor, then waited breathlessly as she listened for the sound of the guest-room door closing behind him.

How had she allowed herself to be talked into giving him a room for the night? And it was only for one night—she had made that very clear to him before agreeing to feed him.

But why had she agreed? A psychiatrist could have a field day answering that question. It certainly wasn't as if Max couldn't afford the price of a room at any of the city's many hotels. What reason could she give herself—give Luke—for allowing her ex-husband to spend the night under the same roof with her? Scratch that—to allow her *husband* to spend the night under the same roof with his *wife*.

Good God, they were still married!

Pulling the covers up under her chin as if to protect herself from being seen, Julia at last came face-to-face with the facts. She was married. To Max. To the man who had come into her life like an answered prayer, only to have the marriage fall apart like a house of cards five months later.

She smiled at the mild metaphor. A house of cards? Hardly. Their marriage had been more reminiscent of life in a mine field, or on a nuclear testing range—beginning with the day she'd told him she wasn't going to use the name Rafferty on the job.

He hadn't given her a chance to explain her reasons, hadn't even given her the chance to breathe, as a matter of fact. No, Max had exploded into a rage, demanding to know if she was ashamed of the name Rafferty, ashamed of him.

It was just like Max to take everything personally, Julia thought, turning onto her side and punching her pillow. He saw everything as it applied to *him,* how it affected *him.*

Even this marriage thing, she decided, picking up another feather pillow and jamming it behind her head. He wanted to be married again—and never mind what she thought. The great Max Rafferty had decreed it, therefore it must be so!

"He loves me," Julia muttered aloud, turning onto her back in yet another effort to get comfortable.

"Love doesn't begin and end in the bedroom. Love comes from the mind as well as the heart. And Max Rafferty wouldn't know real love if it came up and bit him on the—oh, darn it, where's Wellington?"

That's what was wrong; Wellington was missing. Julia might have been able to discourage Wellington from sleeping on the living room furniture—until tonight, at least—but his presence at the bottom of her bed, his warm bulk lying against her legs, had been welcome company.

Throwing back the covers, Julia crossed the parquet floor on tiptoe, unlocked the door and gingerly pulled it open, praying it wouldn't squeak and give her away. The last thing she needed was to have Max believe she was lurking outside his door because she was lonely for him. She'd started down the hall, thinking Wellington must still be in the kitchen, when she heard the deep timbre of Max's voice coming through the guest-room door.

"Now look, mutt, I may have let you in here, but half this bed is mine, okay? And stop kissing me. You smell just like a dog. Have you ever considered breath mints? Good dog, you lay down there. We're going to be great pals, you and me—the men against the women, or in this case, one woman. She's starting to like me again, don't you think so?"

Wellington barked once and Julia's eyes narrowed as she conjured up a vision of the dog sitting on the bed at Max's feet, his tongue lolling and his large tail beating against the mattress as he worshipped his new lord and master.

"That does it," she muttered, stomping heavily back into her lonely bedroom and slamming the door behind her. The large house that she had thought could accommodate three generations of Sutherlands now seemed too confining to hold two people. One of them had to go, and it wasn't going to be her—not this time.

"I need somebody who's on my side. First thing tomorrow morning I ought to go to the mall and buy a cat. *Two* cats! Both of them female—and pregnant!"

The morning dawned brightly, which was a good thing for Max, because the morning also came very early in the form of Wellington scratching at the bedroom door in a bid to get out.

By the time Julia had showered and dressed in a creamy full-length dressing gown that cinched half her slim waist while flowing freely from shoulder blades to heels, Max and Wellington were back from an early-morning run down Hamilton Street and the inviting aroma of frying bacon filled the large Victorian house.

"Ah, the queen has deigned to join us, Wellington," Max said as Julia entered the kitchen to stop and survey the table set with her everyday china, "and just in time to make the toast. You will make the toast, won't you, darling? That always was your job, as I remember."

"Your memory has always been excellent, Max, if selective," Julia replied stiffly, her chin high as she walked past the table, scooped the bread up by its plastic wrapper and headed for the toaster. "I said you could spend the night. I don't recall saying anything about playing house."

Max looked at his wife, at her slim, elegantly erect posture in the jewel-necked dressing gown that gave her the intriguing appearance of a high-fashion nun. A thin white satin band held her deep auburn hair away from her cleanly scrubbed face. She was coolly beautiful and sexy as hell; twice as sexy because she was unaware of the effect her modest gown and regal carriage had on his senses.

"Playing house, Julia?" he responded, deliberately turning his back on temptation. "Honey, if we were playing house it would be night-night time, not breakfast time. Now get a move on with that toast. The eggs are almost ready."

It would be pointless to tell Max she didn't eat eggs anymore. Besides, he'd always had a way with scrambled eggs, cooking them just long enough for them to be light and fluffy without being either overdone or runny. Julia picked up her fork and took a bite as Max sat down across from her.

Suddenly, with the taste of scrambled eggs in her mouth, it was another Sunday morning. Julia was back in their penthouse kitchen and Max was at the stove, dishing out large portions of hash brown potatoes for the two of them.

How she had loved those Sunday mornings when Max took over kitchen duty, plying her with a he-man breakfast that she always swore she couldn't finish, but always did.

And then they'd go into the living room, the one that had one whole wall of glass overlooking Central

Park, and lie side by side on the wide couch while Max read to her from the comic pages. He'd do the voices of all the characters, and she'd dissolve in giggles even before he reached the punch line.

Sooner or later, depending on their mood, they'd adjourn to either the floor or the bedroom and make love, sometimes for hours. Yes, Sundays had been the one day when the two of them were completely compatible, and the memories clutched painfully at her heart, destroying her appetite.

"Hey, you're not eating," Max said, startling her. "Would you rather go into the living room? I picked up the paper from our front porch when Wellington and I came back from our run. Maybe you'd like me to read the comics to you."

Julia stood up so quickly the chair nearly toppled, then she took her plate to the sink. With her back to him, she dumped the food into the sink and turned on the garbage disposal before loading the plate into the dishwasher.

"Thank you, no, Max," she said politely as she turned and headed for the narrow staircase that led upstairs from the kitchen, faltering only as she added, "and it's *my* front porch, not *our* front porch. Please be gone by the time I come back downstairs. You can leave your lawyer's name on the notepad on the refrigerator, and my lawyer will get back to him."

Max whistled a lively tune from a musical he had seen a week earlier in New York as he loaded the remainder of the plates into the dishwasher. It was working. His plan was working. If Julia thought she was going to get rid of him so easily she was going to have to try harder to control her reactions.

Mentioning the comics had been a masterstroke, as had the eggs he'd bought after checking her refrigerator and finding only egg substitute. Julia might talk a good game, but she was far from immune to him.

And, damn it, he was far from immune to her. He could no longer recall what he had expected when he saw her again, but nothing had prepared him for the kick to the gut he'd felt when he saw her standing on the sidewalk, smiling up at the stars.

He must have been out of his mind to ever let Julia go, to let her walk out of his life. Not that he had truly believed she would stay away for long. Oh, no. Besides, he had been too angry to go looking for her, which was as it should have been, because he had been the injured party. Surely she couldn't have expected him to go running after her! All he had to do was wait, and she would come back to him.

But the weeks had dragged on and Julia hadn't made any effort to come home, and Max couldn't bring himself to take the first step.

After all, how many times could a man be hit over the head with the fact that his wife wanted to present herself to the world as unattached, as if ashamed to admit that she was a part of him? He wasn't ashamed of her, for crying out loud. He had always loved to show her off, had been proud of the way men looked at her and the way they envied him.

More than anything, he had loved the way she made him feel. She had been so loyal to him—at least in public—so adoring, so protective of his interests. Although he had always been confident of his own worth, with Julia by his side Max had felt as if nothing was impossible. The world became his oyster, and Julia had been the pearl.

At least that was the way it had been at the beginning. As the months of the marriage had built to three, then four, the luster began to fade, discolored by the arguments.

He was domineering, she had said. He assumed she agreed with him, she had argued, on everything from where they would have dinner to who should be President of the United States. He was too used to having his own way, casting himself as king—a king who wanted nothing more from her than that she be his willing consort as he moved among the common people who bowed respectfully as they passed by.

And what, Max thought now, slamming the lid on the garbage can, was so godawful wrong with that? Hadn't she told him time and again how much she admired his self-confidence, his generosity, his vitality, his strength?

He ran up the back stairs two at a time, heading for the guest room. Oh, sure, she admired all of it. She just didn't want any of it to affect her! "Little Miss Independent," he grumbled, noticing that she had already stripped those ridiculous flowered sheets from the bed, as if showing him silently that he had been dismissed, from her heart as well as her house.

Rooting through his suitcase to unearth his electric razor and other toiletries, Max headed for the bathroom to take a shower, already planning the next move in his campaign.

* * *

"Where is he now?"

Julia subsided into the corner of the couch—the same spot Max had taken for his own the previous evening—and took a sip of coffee. "He's upstairs, packing, if he knows what's good for him."

Luke shook his head, walking to the window to look out on the wide, weekend-quiet Hamilton Street. "I wouldn't want to put money on it, Julia," he warned quietly, his hands jammed deep in his pockets. "Max doesn't strike me as the agreeable type, not when he's after something."

"Or someone," Julia corrected, setting the cup back on the saucer that rested on the coffee table. Luke had arrived fifteen minutes earlier, and she had clung to him as if he were the last remaining bit of sanity in an otherwise wildly unbalanced world. "I want to thank you for not questioning why I allowed Max to spend the night."

Luke turned away from the window, his dark eyes unreadable as he crossed to a chair and sat down. "Max wasn't about to try anything stupid, Julia. I knew that last night. He's too smart to push too far too soon. But don't think you can file for divorce without him putting up a squawk. I don't think the man will ever go down easy."

Julia nodded her agreement. "You're right, of course. I think Max is trying to win me back with the sheer power of his charm. It may have worked once, but it won't work twice."

Luke laughed. "You know, Julia, the weird part about it is that I really think I like the guy. He certainly isn't subtle, is he? I mean, he knows what he wants, and he goes after it. If nothing else, I have to admire his guts.''

"And another one bites the dust," Julia grumbled under her breath. "That's good old Max—everybody's buddy. You can be so blinded by his sunny smile, so overcome with his crackling vitality and openhanded generosity that you don't see until it's too late that you don't exist anymore, unless it's through him.''

"He is rather overpowering," Luke agreed, turning his head as he heard a noise on the stairs. "Put on your armor, darling, I think General Rafferty is about to mount another charge.''

Max entered the living room at a leisurely pace, his fluid, catlike walk calling attention to the casual elegance of his cream wool slacks and black turtleneck sweater as well as his barely tamed mane of tawny hair and bright blue eyes. A gold watch flashed on his left wrist and his genuine smile lighted up the room. "Luke! Good to see you again," he said brightly, advancing toward the other man with his hand outstretched. "Have you eaten, or can I make something for you? Julia and I ate earlier, but it wouldn't be any trouble.''

"No, ordinarily it wouldn't be," Julia inserted smoothly, "except for the fact that Luke and I have just made plans to go out for lunch and then on to the movies.''

"The movies?" Max repeated, neatly skirting the coffee table to sit himself down beside his wife. "That sounds wonderful. I don't remember the last time I saw a movie in a theater rather than renting it after it came out on video. Wait a minute, yes, I do." He took Julia's hand, holding it loosely. "You remember, hon, we saw a James Bond film that day at the shore. It was raining, you understand," he told Luke, "and even newlyweds can't spend the entire day in bed, can they? Yes, it's been almost five years since I've gone to the movies."

Julia, stung into speech, jerked her hand free from Max's grip, longing to slap him silly, whether because of his embarrassing personal remark or his casual show of affection that had a less-than-casual effect on her equilibrium she wasn't sure. "My heart bleeds for you. Please, Max, stop telling us how deprived you are, or I may cry."

Luke picked up the tan trench coat he had draped across the back of the chair earlier and shrugged into it. "We'd take you along with us, Max, except that I have to stop in at Allentown Hospital to check on a surgical patient of mine."

Max was instantly all concern. "You operated on the child? Is he going to be all right?"

"Christopher? He only had a hernia repair," Luke answered, helping Julia into a full-length white wool coat and watching after her as she went to the dining room to get her purse. "And he's going to be fine, although I am worried about him. His mother is little more than a baby herself, unmarried, and without much money. She's great with Christopher, though, and with a few lucky breaks, they'll both be fine. Well, it looks like we're off. Goodbye, Max."

"Yes," Julia said from the archway leading to the foyer, employing a bone-chilling tone of voice that would have sent a polar bear running for a fur coat, *"goodbye* Max."

Max remained on the couch, Wellington having assumed his newly acquired position of comfort, with his head on Max's lap. Max waved at his wife and the doctor as he reached for the remote control to the television. "You two kids have fun now," he answered, switching on the television. "I'm just going to catch up on the news."

As Luke moved into the foyer, Julia stopped to look back over her shoulder just in time to see Max in the act of plunking his sneaker-clad feet on her glass-topped coffee table.

"Right," she muttered, adjusting the strap of her purse as it threatened to slip from her shoulder. "You and that fuzzy Benedict Arnold can just hang out together and watch the news. But if you're still here when we get back, Max, I'm going to be *making* some news, because I'll murder you—film at eleven!"

The minute Max heard the sound of doors closing and Luke's car pulling away from the curb, he shut off the television and was off the couch, the abruptly deserted Wellington looking up quizzically at his new friend.

Rubbing his hands together in what an innocent bystander could only term unholy glee, Max stood in the middle of the living room, congratulating himself on his own brilliance. "The eggs got to her, just as I'd planned, and the reference to our honeymoon can only be considered a bonus. Now, Wellington, my boy, we're ready to move on to Plan B.'' He looked down at his cream slacks to see that they were covered in black doggy hair. "But first I have to change clothes. Mutt, you're just lucky I like you!"

Wellington rolled over onto his back, his paws in the air as he beat at the couch with his tail, obviously delighted to have been of service.

Chapter Four

Julia quietly let herself into the house just after six, closing the door on the March darkness before leaning against the leaded glass pane in near exhaustion.

She'd had a long day Saturday and little sleep last night, so that all she wanted to think about now was grabbing a quick sandwich in the kitchen and heading upstairs to bed.

Luke had promised her dinner after the movie, but his electronic pager had gone off as they were walking to the car, alerting him to an emergency at the hospital. Julia had become used to the insistent beeping of Luke's pager in the months they had been seeing each other, and couldn't find it in her heart to resent it. She had visited the hospital with him more than once and knew his patients needed him.

She smiled as she remembered watching Luke that afternoon with young Christopher Bailey, his manner so gentle and reassuring that the child had barely noticed when Luke had removed the adhesive tape and gauze to examine his incision.

There was a lot Julia liked about Luke, his determination, his dedication, his quiet refusal to go away when she repeatedly turned down his invitations to dinner, until he had penetrated her reserve and made her believe that it just might be possible to find happiness away from Max.

Max. Julia stiffened, sniffing the air as she realized that her stomach was growling in response to a mouthwatering aroma permeating the house.

"Spaghetti sauce," she hissed, untying the belt to her coat as she stormed out of the foyer, taking a shortcut down the narrow back hallway that opened into the kitchen. "Maximillian Rafferty, you rat! I thought I asked you to leave!"

Max, who was in the process of setting the table, turned to look at his wife. "You may have asked, hon, but I don't remember answering. You're home early. I didn't hear the door. You know, Julia, I've been meaning to talk to you about that. You're lucky it was only Luke walking in on you last night. Either lock your door or teach Wellington to bark at intruders."

"Only Luke? What do you mean, *only* Luke? And I'd like to teach Wellington to *bite* intruders—if I didn't think you'd make him sick," Julia said tightly, crossing to the stove to lift the lid of one of the large pots. "Just as I thought! And meatballs, yet! Max, who said you could take over my kitchen?"

"Whoops, water's boiling—excuse me, hon," Max said smoothly, stepping past Julia, a box of spaghetti in his hand. "There are two tossed salads in the fridge—yours is the one without cucumbers. Now, why don't we leave arguing for later, after we've eaten? Where's Luke? I set three places. Did he have an emergency or something?"

Three places? Julia's mouth formed the words silently as she looked at the table. He had set three places. She looked back at Max, who was concentrating on feeding the hard spaghetti into the boiling water. For a guy who had never made any bones about being jealous when they were married, now that she was engaged to another man he was acting like he was bucking for the Nobel Peace Prize. "Yes, um, yes, Luke had an emergency at the hospital," she mumbled, wracking her brain to understand what Max was up to this time.

"It couldn't be Christopher," Max said, opening the oven door to check on the garlic bread he had put in earlier. "What was it, an automobile accident?"

"Skateboard accident. An eleven-year-old with a ruptured spleen or something." Julia removed her coat, hanging it on the hook behind the kitchen door. "Max, how did you know it wasn't Christopher?"

"Simple, hon," he told her easily. "Luke said the boy was fine. And it was only a simple hernia repair, wasn't it?"

Seating herself at the table, Julia allowed her forehead to rest in the palm of one hand. Why had she even bothered asking the question? Max was never wrong. "The sauce smells good," she offered weakly, unable to think of anything else to say. "I should have realized you'd remember my mother's recipe."

Max opened a closet door to take out the spaghetti strainer. He had to have done an inventory of her entire kitchen, Julia realized, for he never took a misstep. She sat up straight, feeling strangely violated.

"How are your parents, Julia? I haven't heard from them since Christmas."

Julia was instantly diverted. How it galled her that Max and her parents still kept up a correspondence, just as if what had happened between her and Max was separate from the affection they held for him. "They're fine. I got a letter Friday from Mother. They're going to the Bahamas this week with some friends who live near them in Orlando."

The spaghetti was on the table in front of her now, as well as a platter piled high with crusty garlic bread. "You must miss them since they moved south. How long is it now, two years?"

"Two and a half—and I go down to see them at least three times a year. Everything looks delicious, Max. Tell me, once you've exhausted your recipes, which you'll do once you fill the entire house with smoke, frying T-bones—*then* will you go away? You're beginning to get on my nerves."

Expertly twirling spaghetti on his fork, Max countered, "I spend all afternoon elbow-deep in meatball mix so that you and Luke can have a nice dinner, and what do I get—sarcasm! That's gratitude for you. Has Luke ever seen this side of you, Julia, or do you save it just for me?"

Julia looked at her filled plate, then down the table at Max. "I doubt you'd look any better in spaghetti and meatballs than you did in linguine with clam sauce," she warned quietly.

Her dart hit home. She could see that it had from the way sudden hot color suffused Max's throat and cheeks. She sat back and folded her arms, waiting for Max The Rocket to lift off. "Ten, nine, eight," she counted softly.

Throwing down his napkin with a vengeance at the count of seven, he rose to begin pacing the kitchen floor. "I don't get it, Julia. I never *did* get it. What's so terrible about a husband resenting the idea that his wife wants to go into business for herself—and without any help from him?"

Julia sat forward quietly, her posture erect, seemingly unmoved by his outburst as she twirled a few strands of spaghetti around her fork. "You don't know how to *help*, Max. You would have taken over the whole business. And you'll never change. Look how you've already taken over my kitchen."

Max raked a hand through his thick tawny hair. "You're my *wife*, damn it! It's my business to protect you, to look out for you."

Julia lifted the fork to her mouth as she looked at him intently, her expression blank and unreadable, saying nothing.

"There you go again, looking straight through me with those damn dark eyes! What are you looking for, Julia? The key to my soul—or the key to my destruction? Do you know what it's like to be on the receiving end of one of those solemn stares? I feel like a moth stuck on a pin, waiting for you to come at me with tweezers to pull off my wings!"

"I'm not staring at you, Max," Julia said at last. "I'm just looking at you. What don't you want me to see?"

He spread his arms, then lifted his eyes to the ceiling, roaring, "Forget it! Just forget I ever said anything! I'm getting out of here before you drive me crazy!"

He was halfway to the door before Julia spoke, her voice low and controlled. "Still the same old Max, aren't you? You're never wrong, just misunderstood. You expect everyone to love you, everyone to listen to you because you're so wise, so much smarter than us mere mortals. Now, after exploding all over my kitchen—and not hearing a word I've said—you're going off to pout."

"I am *not* going off to pout," Max declared hotly. "I'm going for a walk to cool down. Maybe you'll have a better appetite if you don't see my face at the other end of the table." Five seconds later she heard the front door slam so hard the glass pane rattled in its frame.

She shook her head, picking up her fork once more. "If only you'd stay away, Max," she whispered quietly, "but you won't. You can't stand it. You'll be back, wearing a sheepish, lovable smile and probably carrying some silly gift, expecting all to be forgiven—and without offering so much as a single word of apology. That's why *I* had to leave you, Max, because *you* kept coming back."

The moment the door closed behind him, Max knew he had blundered. He had vowed not to explode—

promised himself he wouldn't, last night, and again this afternoon—and had vowed not to quarrel over old hurts. And the first time Julia had turned those dark all-seeing eyes on him he had gone off like a fireworks display on the Fourth of July.

"Good going, Rafferty," he grumbled, searching his slacks pockets for the keys to his car before remembering he had left them on the coffee table. He cursed under his breath. He didn't want to walk, he wanted to drive. He wanted to feel the throb of a powerful machine pulsing beneath his hands as he drove through his anger and his pain.

But he didn't want it enough to go back into the house—not yet. He'd make her suffer first, give her time to regret insulting him by bringing up the linguine incident, waving it over his head as if to declare, "*Ta-da,* I won—you lost!"

With a single searing look back at the house, Max bounded down the porch steps, cut across the winterbrown lawn and headed toward the downtown mall area of the city.

Why did Julia feel such a crying need to dominate him? She had told him long ago that the first thing that had attracted her to him—other than his good looks, she had teased one morning as she perched on the side of the bathtub and watched him shave—was his self-confidence, and his ease in showing that confidence to the world. Self-confidence—what a laugh that was! He had never felt confident around her. He had even nicked his chin with the razor, he remembered now, and he hardly ever cut himself shaving.

Julia was so cool, so collected, so poised and aloof. He had never met a woman who seemed so supremely secure of her place in the world. And her place in the world, she had told him by both word and action, was by his side.

Didn't she know how he envied her the composure she took for granted? Didn't she understand that there were times, so many times, that he felt lost and alone and unworthy? With Julia beside him Max could have conquered the world. He was still making a large dent in it, but without Julia to share his triumphs, to make him glow with her love that had bordered on devotion, his successes had lost much of their excitement.

As his fluid, confident strides ate up the long city blocks, Max plunged further and further into black despair, longing for someone to come lick his wounds so that he would live to fight again. And life with Julia had become a fight in the month before their breakup, a real struggle for survival.

Not that the sex had suffered, he thought, grinning briefly. The passion that had flared between them almost immediately, to burn like an all-consuming flame, had been like nothing Max had ever experienced in his life, before or since.

Julia's near silent, passionate intensity had rocked him to his very foundations, and her dark, usually unreadable eyes had been eloquent with love as they lay together in the calm after the storm.

It was out of the bedroom that their troubles seemed insurmountable. Julia had seemed to have difficulty accepting casual affection or teasing, sometimes reacting with a nervous laugh and at other times push-

ing him away, as if the passionate female of his bed
had developed a puritanical streak with the coming of
the dawn.

Max stopped in front of a small boutique, staring
into the display window without really seeing any of
the variety of goods that crowded the space. If there
was one thing, one single thing, that bothered him
most about Julia, it had to be her silences, the uncomfortable feeling that she had secrets that he would
never be allowed to share.

"So why are you killing yourself trying to get her
back?" he asked himself quietly, already knowing the
answer. If he lived a hundred years, if he searched the
far corners of this earth and beyond, he would never
know another woman who loved him as much as Julia had loved him; another woman who made him feel
that he was the supreme center of her universe. It was
impossible not to love her back. And he did love her;
he loved her so much it hurt.

Having stood his ground for five long years, refusing to be the one who made the first move, he had
shifted gears with a vengeance. He was on the prowl
now, and he wasn't about to turn tail and run at the
first sign of resistance. He had to get Julia back, he
had to have her in his life once more, or the memory
of the woman, already seared into his brain, would
haunt him into eternity.

Shaking his head to rid his mind of such profound
thoughts, Max noticed something in a far corner of the
display window. "Well, how about that," he said
softly, feeling as if the storm clouds were passing and
the sun had come back into his life. "It must be fate."

A slow, satisfied smile curved his lips and he stepped back to see lights blazing in the second-floor windows above the store.

Julia had just finished wiping the kitchen counters when she heard the phone, its muted ring barely audible above the sound of the wash cycle of the dishwasher.

"Hello," she said carefully, lifting the receiver and silently praying it wasn't someone calling to tell her that Max had been injured in an accident—stepping in front of a bus or something as he prowled along, deep in one of his blue funks.

"Hello, darling. Did I wake you? You said you had planned an early night."

Julia raised her eyes to the ceiling, silently berating herself. Why had her first thoughts been of Max, and why had those thoughts included worry for his welfare? He was a big boy, he could take care of himself. He had been doing a good job of it for the past five years, hadn't he?

"No, Luke, I'm not in bed," she said, pulling the handle of the dishwasher to the Off position and sitting down on the high-legged kitchen stool. "Did the surgery go well?"

"Fine, although I'm still at the hospital. Julia, I was down in Pediatrics, writing orders for my new patient, and Marcia Bailey stopped me in the hall. It's the weirdest thing."

Julia stood up, remembering the small blond cherub who was Christopher Bailey. "Is Christopher all right?" she asked hurriedly.

Luke laughed, immediately easing her fears. "All right? I should say so. He looked great—once I could find him. His crib was piled high with stuffed animals. You should see it, Julia, there's a Winnie The Pooh in there that's as big as a small pony."

"I don't understand."

"Welcome to the club, Julia," Luke responded, a scraping noise in the background telling her that he had pulled up a chair and sat down. "Marcia Bailey isn't talking—much."

"Tell me about it, darling." She formed a mental picture of Luke in his wrinkled hospital greens, his dark hair falling onto his forehead as a boyish grin coaxed slashing lines into his lean cheeks.

"I thought you'd be interested. It seems Christopher had a visitor this afternoon, about an hour after we left as a matter of fact. This guy must really have been something, because Marcia is still dreamy-eyed, and I've already had three nurses come up to me to ask if I know him."

Julia felt a sinking sensation in her stomach and was very glad she was sitting down.

"Anyway, this guy played with Christopher for a while, pulling him up and down the hall in the playroom wagon and having a high old time, and then he gave Marcia a whopping check and his business card, just in case she ever needed anything. Now, here comes the kicker. He swore Marcia to secrecy, so she won't tell me his name. Julia," Luke said, pausing a moment, "are you thinking what I'm thinking?"

"Max," Julia said, fighting quick tears as she remembered his earlier assurance that Christopher was fine. "Luke, if I live a thousand years I'll never know what he's going to do next. I guess I shouldn't be surprised, though, because he has always been generous with his money. I just can't believe that he swore Marcia Bailey to secrecy. Max has never been one to hide his light under a bushel."

"How can you know that for sure—if he's done this sort of Santa Claus thing before? Don't be so hard on the guy, Julia," Luke said, so that she lifted the phone away from her ear a moment to stare at it owlishly. Didn't Luke understand that Max was his competition? Was there no one Max couldn't win over with his charm? "It has been five years. As we get older we get wiser, you know."

Julia put the phone against her ear once more, having missed most of Luke's last statement. "Right, Luke," she agreed, not bothering to tell him that at this moment good old Santa-Max was out prowling Allentown, deep in one of his self-pitying sulks. "Max is a wonderful human being and I'd be crazy not to take him up on his offer to resume our marriage. Tell me, do you know any pawnshops when I can get a good price for this diamond I'm wearing?"

"Very funny, Julia," Luke quipped, and she could hear the metal chair scraping once more, telling her that he had stood up. "Max Rafferty may be the greatest humanitarian since Schweitzer, but if he thinks he's getting you back he's going to have to learn to eat through his nose."

Julia laughed, then reminded him, "But, Luke, think of your hands. You're a surgeon and shouldn't take chances with them."

"Don't worry about it, darling," he answered matter-of-factly. "I'll use a baseball bat. Hey, Max has left to go back to New York by now, hasn't he? Whoops—there goes my pager. They probably need me for something in recovery. I'll call you tomorrow at work, Julia, all right?"

A moment later Julia was left holding a phone that buzzed in her ear, the connection between Luke and herself broken, mechanically if not by her design. He had hung up quickly, it was true, but she could have told him about Max if she had really wanted to share the information.

"No," she said to the kitchen at large, turning on the dishwasher once more, "Luke has enough on his mind. Max is my problem, and I'll solve him—" she sighed deeply, falling back onto the stool "—one way or the other."

Chapter Five

Something was tickling her just below the bridge of her nose; something feathery soft and fuzzy. Julia turned toward the back of the couch, her eyes still deliberately closed even though she was awake now, and muttered peevishly, "Wellington, you idiot mongrel, go away. I already fed you."

The tickling persisted, so that she felt her nose begin to twitch, as if she was going to sneeze. She sat up, scrubbing at her face. "Now, look here, mutt—" she began resignedly, only to stop, her eyes widening fractionally for a moment as she blurted, "How did you get in here?"

"Through the door, of course," Max answered congenially, smiling as he walked to the closet to hang up his leather coat. "How do you get in, Julia, down the chimney?"

She swung her long legs to the floor, pushing back her curtain of hair as she concentrated on waking up. Max's return was unfolding just as she had earlier imagined it, with the maddening man full of frisk and acting as if nothing was wrong. She was going to need her wits about her for the next few minutes. "Very funny, Max. I *locked* the door."

He came back into the living room to perch on one corner of the coffee table. "Correction. You locked the *front* door. I came in through the back." He shook his head sorrowfully. "I warned you about that, Julia. It isn't like you to be so careless."

She rose gracefully, pushing her sleeves up to the elbow one after the other as she stepped around Max to gain the center of the room. "I will assume you tried the front door first, so that you saw your suitcase on the porch, all packed and ready for your trip back to Manhattan?"

Max's eyes slid to her right and her shoulders slumped momentarily. Looking behind her toward the dining room, she saw his suitcase sitting on the floor, positively glaring at her. "You're impossible, Max, do you know that?"

He shrugged, spreading his hands. "I try," he said, grinning. "Close your eyes, hon, I've got a present for you."

Julia ran a hand through her unbound hair, the floor-length white dressing gown she had worn that morning and donned again after taking a long bath swirling fluidly around her feet as she spun in a complete circle, her hands raised to the ceiling. "No kidding!" she exploded, knowing she was on the verge of losing her temper. "What is it Max, my very own Winnie The Pooh?"

Max looked puzzled. "What's a Winnie The Pooh?" he asked, rising to reach in his slacks pocket and pull out a rabbit's-foot key chain—the soft, fuzzy item he had used to tickle her into wakefulness.

Julia looked at the key chain. Yes, it was a rabbit's foot all right, and it had been dyed a brilliant blue. "That's my present?" she asked, feeling deflated. Max's presents weren't usually so tacky—although the diamond earrings he had given her for Valentine's Day had come pretty close.

Looking down at the key ring he held in his hand, and then back at her, Max pulled a face. "This thing? No, of course not. I picked this up while I was out shopping this afternoon. I figured I could use it to hold this," he explained, reaching into another pocket and pulling out a key.

Julia took one step backward. "What key is that, Max?"

"I found it hanging on a hook in the laundry room earlier but forgot to get it while the getting was good. I picked it up when I came in. It's the spare key to the front door, if this tag hanging from it is correct." He took a step in her direction, the key and its paper tag dangling from his fingertips. "You'll notice that I called it *the* front door, not *our* front door. I may be slow, but I'm learning."

Julia could hardly contain herself. Wrapping her arms about her waist, as if physically holding in her temper, she accused coldly, "Oh, sure, Max, you're learning. Learning how to be sneaky. God, you should leave your brain to science so that maybe someone can figure out how it works. Who said you could take my spare key?''

Max ignored her, as he was prone to do when he was feeling particularly proud of himself. He walked past her into the dining room to retrieve a plastic bag he had laid on the table. "Here, hon, I found this while I was out. Since you aren't going to be nice and close your eyes, I might as well just give it to you. Sorry it isn't wrapped.''

Julia eyed the plastic bag she recognized as coming from one of the downtown stores as if there was a snake inside it, just waiting to bite her. "The downtown stores are closed on Sunday.''

"They're open until six all this month for the Easter shoppers,'' Max informed her, still holding out the bag.

"You didn't stomp out of—you didn't leave the house until after six," she pointed out warily. "What did you do, Max, break the door down?''

"The owner lives upstairs," he said quickly, as if that explained everything, then added, "look, do you want it or not?''

Did she want the gift? Part of her wanted to fling it in his face, for gifts were no substitute for talking out their problems, trying to find some middle ground where the two of them could both stand, separate but equal.

But another part of her, the part that knew that these gifts were the only apology Max knew how to make, longed to reassure him that he wasn't a bad person and she still liked him. She didn't love him—but she still liked him.

Maintaining a tight grip on her elbows with her crossed arms, she used her chin to motion toward the bag. "What is it? The bag looks heavy. It must really be something if you took the trouble to chase down the owner after closing on a Sunday night."

He didn't say anything, just held out the bag once more, dangling it the same way she would dangle a dog biscuit in front of Wellington to reward him for performing one of his two tricks.

Sensing that she was about to make a very large mistake—and fairly certain that Max didn't want to either shake her paw or watch her play dead—Julia took the bag and walked over to sit on the edge of the couch while she opened it.

"Like it?" Max said a moment later, sitting down beside her as Julia stared at the grapefruit-size glass ball that stood on a deep mahogany wooden base she held in her hands.

Julia bit her bottom lip, recognizing the snow scene delicately captured inside the glass as reminiscent of the ski chalet she and Max had stayed in that long-ago weekend in Vermont. *"Uh-huh,"* she mumbled softly, nodding.

It was impossible to say more. That unforgettable weekend, spent mostly beside a roaring fire, with Max doing the cooking as she curled up on the couch, working on the afghan she was crocheting for their bed in the penthouse in Manhattan, had been haunting her for five long years.

How did he do it? How did Max instinctively zero in on her most vulnerable areas, trigger her memories and emotions so easily, so carelessly, without thought to the way he was destroying her?

"I never finished it," she said softly, refusing to cry, even as she felt Max's arm slip around her shoulders.

"The afghan?" he asked, as if he could read her mind. "No, you didn't. I still have it though, tucked away on the top shelf of one of our bedroom closets. Julia…" He moved fractionally closer to her. "Don't you think we might drive back up there one weekend? I'm sure I can arrange—"

She straightened, easing her shoulder away from his softly stroking hand. "Is John Curley still the doorman?" she asked, hastily changing the subject, which had always been her first line of self-defense when anyone or anything got too close. "He was such a sweet man, always telling me to have a nice day as if he really meant it."

Max's hand was back, doing strange, dizzying things to the sensitive nerves behind her right ear. "John retired a year ago, to Wisconsin, of all places. I would have thought he'd be like your parents and follow the sun. Julia—"

"Oh, I don't know," Julia pursued doggedly, hating to hear the slight tremor in her voice, "I think Wisconsin would be lovely. It's the dairy state, or something, isn't it?"

"Or something," Max agreed, lowering his head to nuzzle the side of her long, slim throat as she perched on the edge of the couch, her head high, her back finishing-school straight.

Julia swallowed, hard, her eyes wide. This was ridiculous! She should move; she should push him away; she should conk him over the head with the snow scene she still held on to tightly with both hands as if it would save her from Max's assault on her senses.

"Max," she began breathlessly, tilting her head to the right so that his lips feathered softly upward, toward her ear. "Max, this is crazy. I'm going to marry Luke. We may be married, legally, but we haven't even seen each other in five years. Oh, please, Max, don't do that."

He had taken her earlobe lightly between his teeth, tugging gently as his tongue caressed her soft, warm skin. She was weakening rapidly, and he knew it. Whatever they had lost, whatever differences and difficulties might still lay between them, they had this in common. His body tautened, anxious for anticipated pleasures.

And then she was gone, leaving him alone on the couch, wondering where he had gone wrong.

He looked up at her, standing in the middle of the room, regal as a queen, as untouched by his passion as an ice maiden presiding over a winter landscape. "Julia, why?" he asked, truly puzzled.

"Why?" she gritted, standing very still. "You have the nerve to ask me why? Max, you really take the cake, do you know that? You waltz in here after five years, tell me we're still married—"

"Tell you I still love you—" Max inserted swiftly, rising to approach her.

"Don't interrupt!" Julia turned away, her dark hair swirling sleekly on her pristine white shoulders.

He leaned against the pillows, spreading his arms on the back of the couch. "Please, Julia, go on. I'm all ears."

"No, you're not, Max. You're all gall—and a mile wide! You try to ply me with scrambled eggs and spaghetti sauce and, and—" she gestured toward the snow scene that lay deserted on the couch "—and *that!* Well, let me tell you something, Maximillian Rafferty, it isn't going to work! Not this time!"

Max raised his eyebrows. "Oh, I don't know, Julia. It was working pretty well a minute ago."

Julia screamed in frustration. It was a short, quiet scream, squeezed out from between clenched teeth, but it was a scream just the same. "Don't flatter yourself, Max," she said sharply, immediately regaining control of herself. The last thing she wanted to do was prove how right he was by losing her temper.

"And that's another thing," she continued, not realizing that she was jumping from subject to subject without rhyme or reason. "You know, Max, I can't figure you out. The Max I married would have decked Luke as soon as looked at him, yet you've been very polite, even setting a place for him at dinner tonight. What happened to the jealous king of the jungle, guarding his territory?"

"Luke's a good man," Max told her, picking up the glass ball and shaking it so that it was suddenly snowing once more in Vermont. "Besides, he's no real threat. You haven't been to bed with him."

Julia felt herself descending to Christopher Bailey's age group and unable to stop her fall. "Oh, yeah?" she countered peevishly. "A fat lot you know, buster."

Max looked up from his contemplation of the snow scene, figuratively pinning Julia to the carpet with the steely blue of his eyes. "Really? Then you have been to bed with Luke?"

"That's none of your business!"

Max smiled, and Julia immediately knew she had blundered. "So you haven't been to bed with him," he said, not bothering to keep the triumph out of his voice. "I didn't think so—or, just like you said, the good doctor would still be picking up his teeth. You're beautiful, Julia, the most beautiful woman I've ever seen, but you aren't wearing that special glow anymore. The quiet, contented glow you wore when we were still together."

She stared at him dispassionately for a full ten seconds, her mind seething, before she spoke. "Always going for the lowest common denominator, aren't you, Max? Sex is not the be-all and end-all you think it is. There has to be a lot more to keep a marriage together."

Max nodded. "Yes, I seem to recall something about that in the marriage ceremony, but I imagine you'll want to refresh my memory."

"Commitment, Max," Julia told him, not caring that he was openly baiting her. "Commitment, not possession. There's a difference. You wanted me to belong to you, as if I were a jewel in your crown. You didn't want me to be a person in my own right, capa-

ble of running my own life, capable of running a
business. Well, don't look now, buster, but I'm doing
a pretty good job of running my life without you!''

"You sure are, hon," Max told her, still sprawled at
his ease—which was rapidly driving her crazy—his
casual posture nonetheless dominating the room. "But
tell me something, Julia. If you're so together, so satisfied with your life and eager to get me out of it—why
are you crying?''

"I am not crying!" Julia's fingers flew to her
cheeks, only to come away wet. "Oh, *go home!*''

"I am home, Julia," Max told her, his voice low.

"Then go to hell!" Julia turned on her heel and
stormed up the steps.

A smug, satisfied smile played across Max's lips at
the sound of her bedroom door slamming shut. He
wasn't sure anymore what round it was in their battle
of wills, but he was certain that this one had gone to
him.

It was after midnight, and still Julia lay on her back
in the wide bed, her gaze riveted on the ceiling. Wellington had come scratching at her door around ten
o'clock to take up his accustomed spot at the bottom
of the bed and even now was snoring softly, his huge,
shaggy body resting against her left calf.

Julia's body tingled inside the mauve silk nightgown, and she had long ago given up the lie that she
was chilled. No, it was a definite tingle, an awareness
of the physical side of herself that she had thought to
be hibernating, if not totally gone.

All Max had done was stroke her neck—that, and take a nibble or two on her earlobe—and the thrill of passion she had felt for him during their marriage had come rushing back, taking her unawares.

Julia had never considered herself to be a particularly passionate person. At least not *that* sort of passion, she amended silently, shifting her left leg before Wellington's weight put it to sleep. Yes, she had always felt a passion for her work, a passion for lost causes, for right triumphing over wrong, instinctively rooting for the underdog, the disadvantaged and the needy.

It had taken Max to open her eyes to personal passion, the deep throbbing need to satisfy and receive satisfaction in return. When they had parted, she truly believed she had left that passion behind, and over the past five years her chaste existence had not bothered her, for she had directed all of her passions into making the Sutherland line the success it was today.

Yes, that was a good idea. She'd think about Sutherland. She had a big day in front of her tomorrow, her first day back at the design table after her fall showing—a triumph she had hoped to savor but that had been cast in the shadows beneath the brilliant glare of Max's appearance on her porch.

She was going to be one very busy lady come Monday morning. As a matter of fact, she had an entire big spring and summer to get through, with no time left over for worrying about Maximillian Rafferty and his gigantic ego.

Luke understood the demands Sutherland made on her time, but he wasn't jealous of that time, or insistent on being a part of it. He had his career and she had hers. It was a good, nonstressful arrangement.

Luke. What would he say when he found out Max was still in town? He wasn't going to be jumping through hoops when he heard the news, she was sure of that much. No, Luke wasn't going to be happy.

Julia used her thumb to rub at the thin gold band holding the marquise diamond on her left hand, remembering the night Luke had slipped the ring on her finger.

He had known all about Max—at least he knew what she had told him—and had promised her that he would never try to own her. He had also promised to love her forever, and she believed he meant every word he said, because Luke had never lied to her.

Not that Max had ever lied to her, she thought, wondering why she felt she had to defend Max, even to herself. Max was nothing if not direct, stating his feelings openly, good or bad.

He was open about everything, as a matter of fact. His happiness, his sulks, his angers, his delights—all were performed on a grand stage, for everyone to see. She'd always admired Max for that openness. He wasn't like her, afraid to show the world what she was thinking or feeling, for fear no one would understand. She had always hated taking center stage, even this past Saturday at the conclusion of the show, when she had taken the runway with her models.

Julia turned onto her side, willing her wandering mind to shut off, so that she could get to sleep. She had to sleep or she'd be less than useless tomorrow morning.

She and Holly would have to get busy lining up fabric orders. They might even have to hire two more seamstresses to help with the finishing work.

Julia sighed, mentally crossing off her planned visit to Florida at the end of the month. Her parents would understand. Luke would understand.

"Max would never understand," she said aloud, the sound of her voice rousing Wellington momentarily, so that the dog stood up, stared at her balefully, walked around in a tight circle a single time and then collapsed onto the mattress once more with an audible groan.

It was no use. Now she was disturbing the dog. If she was going to be able to sleep at all tonight she would have to go downstairs and get it. Lord knew she didn't want to, but she had no choice.

Folding back the covers, Julia sat up, slipped her feet into a pair of backless satin slippers and covered her nightgown with the white dressing gown, tying the sash tightly at her waist. She walked to the door, listening to make sure Max wasn't wandering the hallway, looking for trouble, then opened it and tiptoed past his room.

No light shone out from under the door, so that she knew he was fast asleep, probably with an inane grin on his face. She had heard him come upstairs around eleven o'clock, as he had made considerable noise rummaging through the linen closet outside her door in search of another set of sheets for his bed.

Holding on to the banister, she crept downstairs into the darkness, wondering how Max could so easily put away the cares and upsets of the day and fall asleep with the ease of a guiltless child.

During that last horrible month of their marriage he had often gone to bed before her, leaving her in the living room to stew over yet another argument while he slept the sleep of an innocent, never knowing how close he had come to having a glass of ice-cold water dumped on his head.

Flipping on the light switch, she saw the snow scene resting on the coffee table and sped across the room to snatch it up and return upstairs before Wellington could wake, miss her, and rouse Max with his barking.

Seconds later she was back upstairs, the snow scene sitting on the night table beside her bed, the light coming into her bedroom from the street lamp outside on Hamilton Street making the interior of the glass ball visible in the dark room.

She laid the dressing gown over a chair and crawled back into bed, turning on her side to contemplate the miniature landscape trapped inside the glass ball. The artificial snow still swirled from the shaking she had given it, and she reached over to check the base, having felt something metal sticking out from the recessed circle of wood.

It was a music box; she hadn't known that. She looked toward the door, mentally gauging its thickness and wondering if it would be possible to wind the music box without waking Max. Besides, now that she had the thing in her room, she couldn't possibly go to sleep until she knew what song it played.

In the end, temptation got the better of her and she wound the box with the small gold key, then set it back on the table, lying back to listen to one of Max's favorite songs, tears gathering in the corners of her eyes.

Across the hallway, as he lay propped against the pillows at the head of the bed, his hands crossed behind his head, Max smiled contentedly as the soft tinkling sounds of the title song from *Camelot* reached him through the night.

Chapter Six

Even before the advent of the Civil War, Allentown had been a center of textile manufacture. Fortunes were made during the war by supplying the Union troops with wool uniforms and blankets. Later, a number of silk mills had joined the industry, and although many of the companies either floundered financially in the Great Depression or moved to the southern states, several companies, most of them family-owned, had remained in the area.

Having been born in Allentown, her father working as a master tailor in one of the plants manufacturing men's clothing, Julia had grown up around the industry, and a huge commercial sewing machine, a gift from her father on her tenth birthday, had soon become Julia's most treasured possession.

She had begun designing clothing for her dolls, creating everything from miniature bell-bottom slacks to ornate wedding gowns, slowly finding a happy medium of classic styles and soft, muted colors that she designed and sewed for herself and her friends. There had never been any question in her mind that she would one day design clothing professionally, either for a company or under her own label.

Max had come into Julia's life just as she was about to resign her position as chief designer at a clothing manufacturer in nearby Northampton and launch her own line, which was why she had opted to attend Max's entrepreneurship seminars in the first place.

And that meeting, she thought as she parked her late-model compact car outside the small, one-floor brick building that was the headquarters of Sutherland, Inc., had changed her life in every way.

Snatching up her attaché case, Julia stepped from the car directly into a three-inch-deep puddle left over from the rain that had kept her awake since three that morning. "Oh, great," she grumbled, looking down at her wet foot. "I just love Mondays."

"Talking to yourself, Julia?" Holly Hollis asked, walking across the parking lot to pause beside her employer.

Julia shook her head, following Holly into the building. "I wasn't talking to myself, Holly. I was just saying goodbye to Tom. Tom Cruise, you understand, the movie star. You did see him sitting in my car didn't you, with that pitiful, hangdog expression on his face? He begged me to run away with him to Cancun, but I told him I had to work."

"Right," Holly said, leading the way through the noisy room full of women already working at their sewing machines. "I was with Richard Gere, myself, Saturday night, but when I told him I had to have the limo back by midnight or it turned into a nondeductible pumpkin, he took off."

Waving to her employees as she went, Julia closed the door to her office, leaving the hum of the machines outside, to watch Holly collapse her petite body into the chair behind her desk, a disgruntled expression on her usually cheerful face. After hanging up her coat, Julia subsided onto the small blue velvet loveseat that sat against one wall, removing her left shoe to examine it for water damage, hoping she hadn't gotten a stain on her extremely perishable ivory wool slacks. "May I take it then that Charley's Pub was a lead balloon?" she offered tentatively.

"The only thing taking off Saturday night were the planes flying out of the airport across the street. I would have been better off going to my mother's. At least she would have fed me." She popped a piece of penny bubble gum into her mouth. "So, Julia, how was your weekend?"

"Good question," Julia responded dryly, wondering where to begin. She and Holly had met when Julia moved back to Allentown and began holding interviews for a secretary-cum-general-assistant, and their friendship had grown over the ensuing years, both personally and professionally.

It seemed unbelievable to Julia that she had never told Holly about Max—but she hadn't.

How could she blithely announce now that her weekend had been *all right and—oh, by the way—my ex-husband, Max, showed up unexpectedly Saturday*

*night to tell me that he really isn't my ex-husband;
we're still married, and he loves me and wants me
back, even if he did welcome my fiancé into the house
as if the man were a friend of the family and—oh,
yes—did I tell you, when I last looked, Max was still
sound asleep in my guest bedroom?*

No, she couldn't say that—not unless she was prepared to perform the Heimlich maneuver on Holly
when her friend choked on her bubble gum.

Knowing she had already been quiet too long, Julia
rushed into speech. "I looked through the orders and
I think we definitely have to put on a few extra seamstresses for the duration." She rose to fill the percolator with bottled water, spooned in coffee, and
plugged in the machine, filling the uncomfortable silence with mundane routine.

"Julia?"

"Hmm?" she responded, opening the attaché case
she had laid on her desk. She turned around to see
Holly looking at her oddly.

"Something's up, isn't it?"

"Up? No, of course not." Julia felt her stomach
muscles tighten as the percolator began its usual racket
of hiccuping pops, and the smell of brewing coffee
drifted to her nose. Why did she suddenly feel an almost overpowering urge to call her mother, just as if
she had been transformed into a weepy teenager in
need of comfort? "Why would you think that?"

Holly sat back in the leather swivel chair, twirling a
pencil between her fingers and pushing the chair back
and forth by pressing the tips of her shoes against the
tile floor as she looked assessingly at her friend.

"I *think* it," she pronounced at last, "because you're jumpy as a cat, and because you're avoiding looking in my eyes while you change the subject. Scorpions almost never fidget, and they always change the subject when they don't want to talk about something."

Pressing her palms on the desktop, Julia leaned forward and looked straight at Holly. "There, I'm standing stock-still, looking directly at you. Are you happy now?"

The smaller woman shivered exaggeratedly, feigning fear. "Oh, those dark Scorpio eyes. Somebody's in big trouble. It isn't me, is it?"

"It could be, Holly, if you don't stop spouting all this hocus-pocus nonsense. How long do you plan to be on this astrology kick, anyway?" Julia stood up straight once more, adjusting the soft, hip-length ivory wool unstructured jacket that covered a pale yellow mohair sweater dotted with small, randomly scattered seed pearls.

Holly shrugged. "Probably not too much longer, Julia. I'm an Aries, and once I get good at something I tend to become bored with it—except my work here at Sutherland, of course."

"Well, thank heaven for small favors," Julia muttered good-naturedly. She noticed that the percolator was quiet, and poured cups of coffee for Holly and herself. As she handed Holly a steaming cup she took a deep breath and encouraged, "But, as long as you're interested in it now, tell me what else a Scorpion does."

"Oh," Holly gushed, taking the cup with both hands, "that book was *so* right. You're just dying of curiosity, aren't you, Julia? Part of you hates it with a passion when anyone tries to get too close, and yet another part of you loves a good mystery, and anything to do with the sciences."

"Astrology is a science now, Holly?" Julia quipped, taking her seat at the large drawing table that stood by the window. "I think I'm beginning to be sorry I asked."

Holly ignored this last statement, obviously eager to launch into a recital of everything she had learned about Scorpions. "They're very secretive about their personal lives—at least certain parts of it they don't believe to be anybody's business but theirs," she began, ticking off her information on the tips of her long, ruby-red fingernails.

That statement hit a little too close to home. Julia bent her head, wishing she could concentrate on the half-formed outline for a cocktail dress that was pinned to the design board.

"They're supposed to be loyal almost to the point of adoration with their mates, and are extremely female females—exotically beautiful, in an aloof, hands-off sort of way. You can always recognize a Scorpion by looking deeply into their eyes. If the look you get back is steady and unwavering and makes you flinch as if the person can see into your soul, you're looking at a Scorpion."

Julia had a flash of memory, hearing Max's voice as he cursed her for her all-seeing dark eyes. Of course, he had seemed to like the way she looked at him in bed, when they were—"Go on," she urged quietly.

"Of course, everybody always jokes about the seductive passion of Scorpions, but that passion isn't reserved only for the bedroom, although everything I've read seems to imply that Scorps make excellent lovers. They're just as passionate if they're trying to save whales, or do the *New York Times* crossword puzzle in ink, or find their lost car keys."

This was beginning to get very scary. Julia picked up a pencil but did not have the faintest notion what she was going to do with it.

Holly was on a roll now, continuing, "Scorpions love being the boss, even if they aren't bossy, and they are usually even-tempered—unless you step on their tail. Their tail! Get it, Julia—tail, Scorpion. Oh, never mind. Scorpions are also known for their unexpressive expressions. Is that a contradiction in terms? Anyway, I'm sure you're laughing like crazy right now on the inside."

"Roaring my head off," Julia agreed, her features set and a little pale. Couldn't the phone ring or something? Holly's happy prattling was beginning to make her feel like some sort of two-legged Pavlovian dog, responding to the preordained stimuli of the stars.

Holly stood, crossing to the percolator to pour herself a second cup of coffee. "Now let's see, I think that about covers it. No, I forgot. Scorpions not only get mad, they get even, usually considerably more than even. I mean, an angry Scorpion isn't happy until they've paid you back at least double for any kindness or any injury."

First thing tomorrow morning I ought to go the mall and buy a cat. Two cats! Both of them female—and pregnant! Julia flinched inwardly, remembering her planned revenge on Wellington and Max the night she had discovered the dog's desertion of her for a new master. She had to admit that she did tend to give back at a rate of at least two to one, but she had to do that so that nobody tried to hurt her a second time. That didn't make her odd, did it?

"Is that it?" she asked, rushing into speech. "I mean, this book you've read makes me sound like a first class nut case."

Holly shook her head. "You've got it all wrong, Julia. Did you know there have been more United States Presidents born under Scorpio than any other sign? Wait a minute. I've got the book about it right over here in my desk."

Julia took a sip of her rapidly cooling coffee while she waited for Holly to page through the book looking for something. "Have you ever considered therapy, Holly?" she asked, her lips twitching as she saw that many passages in the book had been highlighted with a fluorescent yellow marker.

"Spoilsport," Holly groused good-naturedly. "You're just angry because I'm right. Here we go— Scorpio. Yes, it mentions that bit about the Presidents, and there's a list of famous Scorpions."

She read silently for a moment, then gave out a low whistle. "Wow, you're in good company, Julia. Marie Antoinette, Richard Burton—oh, I loved him, didn't you?—Douglas MacArthur, Prince Charles, Pablo Picasso, Grace Kelly, Katharine Hepburn—I *adore* her work—even Jonas Salk! I've got Van Gogh and Charlie Chaplin as fellow Aries, if you can figure that out.''

''Let me see that silly book,'' Julia said with a trace of impatience, taking the slim volume from Holly's hands. She turned back to the beginning of the section that supposedly described Scorpions. ''It says here that my positive characteristics are my independence, my determination and—''

When Julia hesitated, Holly grabbed the book. ''And your *passion*. See, I told you, Julia. And your not so great characteristics are that you want to dominate—although you hide that part of you—you can be vindictive—that's the revenge thing—and you can be *very* sarcastic.''

''Who, sweet little old me?'' Julia quipped, a hand going to the simple, hammered gold chain that hung around her neck.

Holly looked up at her employer. ''Thank you for that, Ms. Sutherland, and I rest my case.'' Obviously feeling she had been justified by the similarities between the book's description of a Scorpion and her friend, she placed the open book on the desk.

The phone rang, too late to save Julia as she had hoped, and Holly busied herself answering a question from one of their jobbers as Julia stood very still, trying to read something from the upside-down book.

Right at the beginning of the chapter it listed the zodiac signs with which Scorpio was supposed to be most compatible: Cancer and Pisces and, to a lesser extent, Capricorn and Virgo. If her memory was correct, there were twelve signs of the zodiac and she was only compatible with four of them. As a matter of fact, according to Holly's handy dandy little book of knowledge, she wasn't even expected to get along too well with herself.

When Holly hung up the phone, Julia asked casually, "What sign of the zodiac represents July?"

"July? It depends. Up to the twenty-third, it's Cancer, and after that it's Leo, the lion. Why do you ask?"

Julia shook her head, returning to the design table. "No reason. I guess Leo and Scorpio aren't very compatible?"

"Leo and Scorpio?" Holly threw up her hands as if to protect herself. "I wouldn't want to be around when those two got together, at least not without a bulletproof vest!"

Julia propped her chin on her palm, allowing a curtain of hair to hide her expression. Why had she thought she needed confirmation from Holly that she and Max were incompatible?

Max sat on the side of Julia's neatly made queen-size bed, holding the glass-domed snow scene between his hands, when the telephone on the night table began to ring. He had turned off the answering machine in Julia's home office earlier, after missing a call from his secretary.

"Rafferty residence," he growled into the phone, disliking the interruption, for he had been lost in a memory of him and Julia in Vermont, and the way they had snuggled in front of a roaring fire, picking out names for all the children they were going to have someday. "Rafferty residence," he said again, not really hearing the person on the other end of the line. It would never occur to him that Julia considered the house to be the "Sutherland residence."

The call came from his office in New York, and Max made short work of settling a few problems that had arisen over the weekend by assigning half a dozen tasks to his most trusted vice president and instructing his private secretary to call his housekeeper and have her pack some of his clothing and express them to him in Allentown.

That dealt with, he set the snow scene back on the table, the mood broken, and left the room, conquering the impulse to open the door of Julia's closet to satisfy himself that none of Luke Manning's clothing hung inside. He really didn't need any further confirmation to comfort him.

He had slept late that morning, probably because he had been awake half the night, considering his next move. Julia had left a place set for him in the kitchen and a variety of dry cereals for him to select from—as well as a pithy farewell note that had wished him a safe trip back to Manhattan.

After crushing the note into a ball and tossing it into the garbage can, he had taken Wellington for a long run in a park he had discovered the night before while he walked away his anger. On his return he had showered, changed into a pair of casual slacks and a turtleneck sweater, and prowled the empty house, seeing Julia's fine touch in every piece of furniture, every perfectly matched color scheme, every figurine and framed picture, keeping her bedroom for his last stop.

Now, sitting in the living room once more, Wellington at his feet, Max wished Julia hadn't made such a rousing success of the years spent away from him, not that he would have been happy if she had fallen on her face. It was just that if Sutherland had failed, she may have come back to him, or he could have gone to her to offer his assistance.

But her venture into self-proprietorship had been successful, and a small article in the morning newspaper today had described her latest triumph in New York. He wasn't surprised that she had done well, and had been following her career ever since she left him, but the knowledge didn't do a whole lot for his ego.

"She's doing well because I'm a damn good teacher," Max told the snoring Wellington, his words sounding hollow and vain, even to his own ears.

Maybe he was pushing Julia, going too fast too soon, and should transfer himself to a local hotel, to wage his campaign while maintaining a little distance from her. He shook his head, dismissing the idea as cowardly. Julia was his wife, and he'd be a fool to leave the scene so that she and Luke Manning could be alone, sit together on this couch, and—

Max leapt to his feet to pace the length of the Oriental carpet, racking his brain for inspiration. He couldn't stand being cooped up inside the house. He was a man of action, not introspection. He couldn't play the waiting game; he wasn't built for it. If he had a problem, he would stalk it for just so long, studying its strengths and locating its weaknesses—and then he would pounce!

And just who did Julia think she was, dismissing him with a box of cereal and an impersonal goodbye note? Did she really believe she could get rid of him so easily? Did he mean that little to her?

Max banished the unwelcome thoughts, replacing them with the memory of the way she had come close to melting in his arms last night, here in this same living room. Yes, he had to stay near her, to keep reminding her of all they'd had, of all they could have again.

But that didn't mean he had to sit here all day, did it, like some retiree waiting for the hours to pass? God, another few hours of all this great peace and tranquility and he would be forced to turn on the television set, to watch soap operas or game shows or some such drivel.

Whistling to Wellington, he walked to the foyer to get his coat and the dog's leash, as he felt suddenly inspired. He would go to Julia's office, dog in tow, and inspect the place for himself. Julia might not like to see him, but she wouldn't throw her own dog out into the cold.

He was just about to hook the leash to Wellington's collar when the phone rang again.

"Rafferty residence, who's this?" he growled imperiously, impatient with any interruption that might keep him from putting his plan into action.

"Max? Can that be you, dear? Yes, of course it is. I thought I'd get Julia's machine. What are you doing there?"

Max smiled, instantly sunny once more at the sound of Margaret Sutherland's surprised greeting. "It's me all right, Margaret. How's Jim doing? Julia told me you two jet-setters were heading for the Bahamas, or is that next week?''

''We're not heading anywhere right now, Max,'' Margaret told him, and Max noticed that the woman's voice sounded rather thin, as if she was under some sort of strain. ''I'm calling from the hospital, which is why I didn't try to reach Julia at work. I can't remember that number off the top of my head.''

Max shushed Wellington, who was beginning to bark, impatient to be outside. ''Did you say the hospital, Margaret? What's the matter with Jim?''

Margaret began to cry. ''That's just it—I don't know! He seemed just fine this morning, but then he said his left arm felt numb and tingly, and then the pain started in his chest, and I insisted we go to the hospital. At first they thought it must be his heart, but now—oh, Max, I'm so glad you're there. I don't want Julia to be alone.''

Thankful it was a cordless phone, Max made for the kitchen and the notepad Julia had left on the table. ''Now listen to me, Margaret. Everything is going to be all right. What's the name of the hospital, and the number you're calling from? All right, I've got it. You just stay calm and Julia and I will be there as fast as we can.''

He could hear Margaret taking a deep, steadying breath. ''Thank you, Max, dear. Since you're there with Julia, I feel better already, and Jim will be so pleased.''

After saying goodbye to Margaret, Max located Julia's personal phone book and made several quick phone calls, then raced upstairs to ransack her bedroom, grabbing clothing suitable for Florida in March and piling it into a suitcase he found in the back of her walk-in closet. Gathering up his own suitcase, he returned to the living room to see Wellington standing there, his tail wagging, the leather leash held between his jaws.

"Oh, great. What am I going to do with you, mutt?" he asked in exasperation, smiling as Wellington tipped his head to one side and looked up at him as if trying to understand Max's question. "Right," Max declared, coming to a decision, and went back into the kitchen, Wellington tagging along at his heels, to look through Julia's personal phone book one more time.

Five minutes later he was on his way downtown, trying to think of the best way to tell Julia about Jim without scaring her.

Chapter Seven

Julia and Holly had been working for three hours, each silently and efficiently dealing with any lingering old business so that, with any luck, by lunchtime their desk would be clear to begin wrestling with the various setup procedures for implementing production on the fall line.

Accustomed as they both were to the noises of the sewing room, both Julia and Holly looked up when a sudden silence, followed by a rush of excited feminine voices, filtered into their office.

"It's not lunchtime yet, is it?" Julia questioned, checking her watch.

"You don't think anyone has sewed themselves to their machine?" Holly asked, wincing. "If someone has, Julia, it's your turn to go look. I thought I'd pass out when I saw that kid, Rose Masterson, the day she—uh-oh, someone's knocking on the door. See, ya, sport, I'm off to check the storage room for paper clips."

"Coward," Julia said, reaching for the first aid kit she kept in her desk. "Besides, Rose is just fine now. I'm coming," she called, heading for the door.

The door opened before Julia could get there, and young Rose Masterson, her eyes wide, poked her head inside. "Ms. Sutherland, there's a man and a dog out here to see you. Lordy, but he's gorgeous. The man, that is, not the dog. Ms. Sutherland—he says he's your husband!"

"Her husband? Who's her husband?" Holly squeaked, her questioning gaze flying to Julia.

"The man, that is, Holly—not the dog," Julia said calmly, her face unreadable as she replaced the first aid kit in the desk. "Thank you, Rose. You may ask him to come in if you want."

"I'd like to ask him a lot of things," Rose declared feelingly, "except he belongs to you. Does he have a brother? Guess not. I'll bring him in as soon as I can pry the rest of the girls off him." Sighing, Rose closed the door behind her.

Julia stood very still, her only movement that of running a hand through her hair so that it rearranged itself sleekly about her head. "Don't," she warned as Holly seemed about to burst into speech. "Don't say a word."

Holly pressed her hand to her breast. "*Me?* Julia, don't be silly. Why should I say anything? Just let me ask one question, one *teensy weensy widdle* question. Seeing as how the girls have all seen Luke—so it can't be him out there—does Luke know about this husband we're going to be meeting?''

"He knows," Julia informed her tersely, nodding once as the door opened. "Hello, Max. Wellington. What brings you down here?''

Max walked across the room, took hold of Julia's shoulders, and kissed her on the mouth, a short, hard kiss that Julia took as Max's way of branding her as his possession. Yet she wasn't angry, for the kiss had seemed to convey something else as well, as if Max had been trying to give her some of his strength.

He turned away from her to address Holly, his smile warm and sunny. "Hello," he said affably, holding out his hand. "I'm Max Rafferty, Julia's husband. We were married five years ago but we sort of lost touch with each other for a while. And you must be Holly, Julia's good right hand."

"Holly Hollis," Holly answered dazedly, shaking Max's hand while staring up at him, openmouthed.

Julia watched as her friend visibly melted beneath the heat of Max's brilliant presence. From the top of his tawny, windswept head to the tips of his custom Italian leather shoes, Max radiated life and vitality. Suddenly, although it was still March outside, it was the height of summer inside the office.

"You always did have a way with entrances, Max," Julia commented dryly, leaning down to pat Wellington affectionately.

"Holly Hollis?" Max questioned, ignoring Julia's remark. "Was that on purpose?"

It took a lot to bowl Holly over, but Max had done it. "Uh-huh," she agreed, watching as Max perched himself on the edge of Julia's desk. "We're all *H*s—my parents, my brothers Herb and Harry, and my sister Helen. Terrible, isn't it?"

Max picked up a silver paperweight in the shape of a large thimble, fingering it idly as he spoke. "Terrible? For someone else, perhaps, Holly, but I think it suits you perfectly. Perky, refreshing—you know what I mean. Holly," he said, and Julia felt her stomach muscles tighten, "do you think you could possibly excuse us for a few minutes? Julia and I have something to discuss."

"I'll bet you do!" Holly answered, rapidly gathering up the papers she had been working on before Max's appearance.

Julia fought the urge to physically restrain her assistant from leaving the room, but she knew Max had already outflanked her. If the look in her eyes meant anything, Holly would swim the Atlantic Ocean for Max, no questions asked.

"And would you please take Wellington with you?" Max held out the looped end of the leash and Holly took it. She stopped directly in front of Max only long enough to take one more look into his startlingly blue eyes and cast a quick, inquiring glance at Julia before heading for the main sewing room and the small crowd of women waiting to pump her for any information she had learned.

Julia sat back in her chair. "Okay, Max, your audience is all gone now, although I guess I should thank you. I mean, you didn't hire a brass band, did you? Is playtime over yet?"

"Margaret phoned a little while ago, hon," he told her without preamble, his face solemn as he looked directly into Julia's eyes. "Your dad has been taken to the hospital."

Julia's dark eyes widened slightly. Of all the things she had thought she might hear, Julia hadn't expected anything like this. She sat very still, absorbing the news. "Heart attack?" she asked Max after a moment, surprising herself with the calm, controlled tone of her voice.

Max shook his head. "They've already ruled that out, hon, but they haven't told Margaret more than that. I've got reservations, nonstop from here to Orlando, on the one-thirty out of the Allentown-Bethlehem-Easton Airport. Our luggage is in my car. We can grab a bite to eat at the airport. You okay?"

Julia reached for the telephone. "I'm fine, Max. I just want to call Luke."

"I already did. He's in surgery, so I left a message with his service. I also gave him your parents' phone number so we can stay in touch."

Julia's hand dropped to the desktop. "You—you phoned Luke? That was very thoughtful of you, Max. Very thoughtful."

"Right," Max said, looking around the room until he located the clothes tree where Julia had hung her coat that morning. "I called the kennel you use for Wellington and I'm sure Holly will agree to drop him off there after we leave. I turned down the heat, poured the milk down the sink, stopped the newspaper and notified the police we'll be out of town indefinitely. Did I forget anything?"

"Only my plants," Julia mumbled quietly, allowing Max to help her with her coat. "Holly will take care of them." She allowed herself to lean back against his strength for just a moment. "I want to thank you for taking charge like this, although I'll probably resent it later, once I can think again. Max—"

"Jim will be just fine, hon. I guarantee it." Max bent forward and kissed Julia's cheek as her voice faltered and she stopped talking, refusing to give in to emotion.

"You guarantee it?" Julia laughed shortly, pulling away from him. "How can you guarantee it?"

"Double your money back if you're not completely satisfied. Come on—it's time we got this show on the road."

The strange thing was, Julia realized in silent amazement, she believed him. Max had a way of making you believe he could do anything. She felt herself relax, willing to allow Max to lead the way.

It only took a minute to explain everything to Holly, who immediately told Julia not to worry about anything for she, Holly, could "run this place with one hand tied behind my back."

"Thanks, Holly," Julia managed to tease. "You make me feel so indispensable."

But Holly wasn't listening. She had run into the office and was back a moment later, just as Julia stepped outside into the gray March day. "Max," Holly called softly, motioning him to her side. "Please don't think I'm being nosy, but are you a Leo?"

Max looked down at the young woman, his blue eyes twinkling. "Is it that obvious?"

"Obvious? If I were a doctor making a diagnosis, I'd say you were a textbook case! Here," she said, pushing the paperback astrology book into his hand. "Give this to Julia once you're in Florida. It may help."

He shook his head. "You've lost me," he admitted, looking at the book.

"*You're* lost? Hey, until you walked in that office, I didn't even know Julia was ever married before. I mean, she's engaged to marry Luke Manning. You're really her ex, right?"

"It came as quite a surprise to us as well, come to think of it, so don't feel all alone. It's a long story, Holly, but no, I'm not her ex. I'm still her husband, even if she only found out a few days ago, and I plan to go on being her husband. She may wear Luke's ring right now, but Julia's mine."

Holly bit her bottom lip. "I like Luke, he's a great guy, but Scorps pretty much mate for life, and if I were in Julia's shoes I'd think twice about letting you get away again."

Max leaned down to kiss Holly on the cheek, then straightened. "If you think it will help me, sweetheart, I'll read this book cover to cover myself," he told her, winking. "I am in here, aren't I? That's why you want Julia to read it, right?"

Holly nodded, blushing. "But you have to promise not to read it yourself. You already seem to know what you want. Just leave the book where Julia can find it. Promise?"

"Max, are you coming?"

He turned to see Julia standing at the door, looking as cool and composed as ever. To an outsider it would appear that she was totally under control, and perhaps even indifferent to her father's condition. But Max knew better. Her entire being was concentrated on getting herself to Florida just as soon as humanly possible.

"Coming, hon," he said, absently pocketing the book in his coat as he headed for the doorway, leaving Holly behind to explain everything to a roomful of inquiring minds that wanted to know just what was going on with their boss.

Max watched as Julia picked at the food on her tray, pushing the creamed green vegetable to the far side of her plate as if she didn't want it to contaminate the two slices of roast beef that lay smothered in slowly congealing gravy.

"Not exactly *cordon bleu,* is it?" he quipped as she laid down her plastic fork.

"More like cardboard bleu," she answered dully. "I hate airline food. I've heard people refer to it as plastic, but it reminds me more of soggy polyester. I guess it's because I like to deal in the real thing." The plane hit a small air pocket and Julia looked out the side window, seeing only gray skies and one silver wing. "How much longer?"

Max checked his watch, then reached across to take her hand, squeezing it reassuringly. He was still amazed at how well they were working together—and not fighting each other—but then they always had seemed to be at their best when they were united in fighting the world rather than each other. "Not much more than an hour. Maybe even less, thanks to this wind that's giving us such a bumpy ride. I've already arranged to have a car waiting to drive us to the hospital. But I told you that already, didn't I?"

Julia nodded. "And you also told me you got hold of Mother while I went to the ladies' room before we left and she said Dad wasn't in any real danger. So why do I feel like standing up in this miserable sardine can and making a complete idiot out of myself by screaming my silly head off?"

Max chuckled low in his throat. "Go ahead, hon, I won't stop you. I may not tell anyone that I know you, but I won't stop you."

"Rat," Julia sniped, turning to smile at him. "Tell me what you packed for me."

Max shrugged. "I don't know. A couple of frilly things, a couple of cotton sweaters, one of those capes you like, some slacks, and some shoes."

"And my toothbrush? My makeup? My hairbrush and shampoo?"

He dismissed such mundane things with a wave of his hand. "We can pick all that stuff up at a store once we're there."

"Oh, Max, you never change. Just deal with the big things and the rest can take care of itself. You may call your assistants 'vice presidents,' but they always reminded me of little janitors in three-piece suits, following you around with push brooms. While you wheeled and dealed, they cleaned up the details after you. Do you remember our honeymoon? You packed

three suits, four pair of slacks, a half dozen shirts, and
not a single pair of socks."

"Hey, we eloped, remember? I was in something of
a hurry. Besides, although I know this will come as a
shock to you, hon, not everyone makes detailed lists
for everything from groceries to spring cleaning proj-
ects."

Julia, undaunted by his teasing, leaned down to pick
up her purse, extracting a pen and a small notebook.
"Speaking of lists," she said, flipping open the notebook, "I ought to jot down some instructions for
Holly while I have time. I can phone her tonight once
we're back at Mother's."

Max lifted his drink, the ice cubes clinking against
the side of the glass as the airplane hit another air
pocket. "Speaking of your *mother,* hon," he began,
hiding a smile.

"Yes?" Julia listened with only half an ear, her
mind already concentrating on instructions concerning the purchase of fabric from one of their southern
suppliers. It was easier to think about fabric orders
than the fact that her very vital father was lying ill in
a hospital bed and her mother was all alone and most
probably frightened nearly out of her mind.

"I think she might be laboring under a slight misunderstanding concerning us."

Julia lifted her head to look at him. She didn't like
the tone of his voice. It sounded entirely too happy, for
one thing, and she now saw that he was looking especially pleased with himself. "A misunderstanding?
What kind of misunderstanding? About us? Maximillian Rafferty, what did you tell her?"

He put up his hands, as if in self-defense. "Nothing. I told her nothing. I just answered the phone and Margaret took it from there. I'm totally innocent in this, honest."

If looks could kill, Max would still be flying at thirty thousand feet, only he would be doing it minus one airplane. "She thinks we've reconciled?" she asked, her voice slow and careful. "Well, don't just sit there grinning like Wellington does after he has chewed another slipper—does Mother think we've reconciled?"

"Does Margaret think we're back together, living as man and wife, madly in love and apt to give her grandchildren sometime soon?" Max folded his hands across his chest. "Yes, I would think that about sums it up."

The notebook slammed closed. "Oh, Max, how could you? And I suppose she's delighted. No, no, don't bother saying anything. She's over the moon. You always could wrap Mother right around your finger. Dad, too. *Dad!* Do you think she'll tell him?"

"After my conversation with Margaret before we took off for Allentown, I'd say she already has. And, according to Margaret and the doctors, Jim perked up as soon as he heard the news."

Julia slumped against the seat. "I think I'm going to be sick."

"Oh no you're not, Julia. I didn't plan this, and I don't want to take advantage of it, but we have to think of your father now. You're going to walk into Jim's hospital room on my arm, and you're going to be bright and smiling and happy."

"And what are *you* going to be, Max?" Julia asked, not liking the look on his face.

"Me?" Max smiled at the stewardess who was bringing him another drink. "I think, my darling wife, that I am going to be very, very smug. Would you like another glass of diet soda?"

Chapter Eight

Max felt the Florida sun warm his face as he led Julia outside the airport terminal, quickly locating the hired car that would take them to the hospital. He had seen the many admiring glances Julia had garnered as they passed through the terminal and still gloried in the same secret elation he'd always experienced when she walked by his side.

He couldn't remember a time he hadn't been proud of Julia, whether they had stood side by side at a party or walked alone, hand in hand along some sandy beach or country path. She made up his other half—his better, honest, loyal self—and he had been incomplete until she'd entered his life.

How had he possibly functioned during the five years they'd been apart? How had he gone through the everyday motions of living, without Julia there to share in his every hurt, his every triumph?

Max had to believe that Julia felt it too, this completeness, that she recognized they belonged together. She had to realize how well they suited each other, how seamlessly they worked together in times of need, of crisis, and how, together, they could take on the whole world.

Granted, Julia had a way of bringing out all the worst in him as well, he acknowledged silently, trying his temper with her steadfast demands to be independent, just as if she felt resentful of his overwhelming desire to protect her. Yet she was clinging to him now, while her father was ill, and hadn't seemed to resent the fact that he had taken charge.

She needed him right now; she relied on his strength, and he wasn't going to let her down. But could he in good conscience take advantage of her momentary weakness, her vulnerability, to worm his way back into her good graces? Could he be so low as to use Jim Sutherland's sudden illness as a way back into Julia's heart?

It wasn't, after all, as if he had planned for Jim to become ill. No, he had just been in the right place at the right time. There was no sin in that, was there? And if Luke Manning couldn't be with her when she needed him, that didn't mean that Julia should have to go through this alone, should it?

They sat side by side in the back of the limousine, Julia's hand tucked confidently in his as each turn of the wheels took them closer to the hospital. She didn't say anything, but Max knew that she was silently thanking him for being with her.

Max felt like a cheap opportunist, and he didn't enjoy the feeling. He didn't need outside influences to get Julia back, to get his wife back where she belonged, in his house, in his arms, in his bed.

All right, so the snow scene had been a determined calculation to remind Julia of that weekend in the cabin. But it was one thing to employ props; it was quite another thing to use Jim's illness.

Max squeezed Julia's hand, prepared to tell her that he would take Margaret to one side and explain the little misunderstanding that had his in-laws believing he and Julia had reconciled. All wasn't fair in love and war, not when it came to Jim's health.

Max was about to open his mouth, about to tell Julia that he'd take a room at a nearby hotel, giving her room to breathe, room to think, when his fingers touched Luke Manning's marquise-cut diamond ring—and the words died in his throat.

His jaw hardened. His wife was engaged to marry another man. His wife had been doing her darnedest to remove him from her life. His wife wasn't going to give him a snowball's chance in hell of winning her back—not unless he could find some way to remind her of all they'd once had together.

All wasn't fair in love and war? Max let go of Julia's hand in order to put a comforting arm around her shoulders as they approached the hospital. The hell it wasn't!

Julia was fighting for her life in the rear seat of the stretch limousine and she knew it. Max's casual embrace was so comforting, his strength so seductive, his air of confidence and command so nearly over-whelming, that she longed for nothing more than to melt against him, hiding within the shelter he seemed so willing to provide.

It would be so easy. Max would take care of every-thing.

He would summon the doctors and demand they perform any miracle that might be necessary to bring her father back to his usual good health.

He would charm the nurses, the orderlies, even the housekeeping staff, until Jim Sutherland's wishes became their paramount reason for being.

He would wrap both Margaret and herself in the safe, warm cocoon of his magnificent omnipotence, banishing all fears, all nameless demons, any lingering hint of fear.

Nothing could go wrong when Maximillian Rafferty was on the scene. No one would dare allow anything to go wrong, because they knew that they would feel the fiery wrath of his righteous anger. If Max said everything was going to be fine, then everything damn well better be fine!

Julia didn't believe she was weaving heroic day-dreams about her husband, and she didn't truly believe he was infallible or incapable of an occasional defeat. It was just that she had seen Max in action before, and she knew how he operated. He operated, simply, from strength. Strength of will, strength of his convictions, the strength that flowed so naturally from his supreme confidence in the rightness of any objective he had in view.

Max had always been just slightly larger than life, appearing in her orbit like some romantic hero out of an epic novel, with goals and ideals and dreams that made her want to believe everything was possible.

Yes, that was it. Max was a hero—and every woman wanted a hero. Hadn't it been that confidence, that strength, that willingness to allow the world to see exactly how sure of himself he was that had drawn her to him in the first place?

And hadn't it been those same attributes that had also angered her, and nearly smothered her and, in the end, driven her away? Wasn't it true that if Max was confident, he could also be arrogant, and that his desire to protect his own could at times verge on tyranny and actual domination?

So, when her father was back out on the golf course, and her mother was once more in her beloved kitchen, mixing up batches of brownies, and the sun was back in its sky—then what?

How could Julia put herself and her family into Max's loving care, then pull away once he had worked his magic? It would be like slapping Wellington for bringing her slippers to her after a long, hard day. Max would expect and deserve a reward, and she knew exactly what Max had in mind.

Poor Max, Julia thought, knowing how badly he would be hurt. And poor Julia, she added, sighing, for if leaving Max once had been difficult, leaving him a second time could destroy her.

She would have to deal with that later, however, for right now the most important thing in her world was her parents.

Julia looked forward to see that the limousine was approaching a large white building that had to be the hospital, and her stomach tightened into an uncomfortable knot. What would they find when they got to her father's room? Max had told her that a heart attack had been ruled out, that her father was in no immediate danger, but she wouldn't really believe it until she saw Jim for herself.

She spent a moment wishing Luke Manning was beside her, his medical knowledge at the ready to help her sift through the technical explanations the doctors would give them.

Luke. Julia bit her bottom lip, feeling guilty that this was the first time she had thought of her fiancé since hearing about her father. Luke was a doctor, and she knew he was a good one, compassionate and caring, and every inch the professional. But did she really want his cool, impersonal detachment when her father was the patient?

No, she realized with a small thrill of shock. She didn't want Luke right now. She wanted Max. She wanted Max's fire, Max's vibrant, demanding presence, Max's pull-out-all-the-stops personality steamrolling over medical protocol and unpronounceable medical jargon as he made it very clear that Jim Sutherland was a part of him, Max Rafferty, and he had damn well better get the best attention and care possible or Max Rafferty would know the reason why!

Julia sneaked a look at Max as he leaned over to open the door as they pulled under the canopy at the hospital entrance. Oh, yes, Max was primed and ready for battle. He'd be strong but generous as he allowed the doctors to talk, then turn on the charm that would have everyone running in circles to please him, even if they couldn't understand why they were doing it.

He'd put his arms around Margaret, unselfishly lending her his strength, tease Jim into laughing at one of his jokes, wink at the nurse so that she would make it a point to check on Jim's condition every few minutes, and find out exactly what was going on before he had been in the hospital half an hour.

Julia knew Max was not some sort of god, or a miracle worker. If her father was truly in trouble, even Max couldn't fix it with the simple power of his overwhelming protective instincts. But he was quite a magician, with an impressive bag of tricks, and right now Julia would rather have him by her side than anyone she could think of—including Luke Manning. Max's performance might, if her father truly was in no danger, even be a lot of fun to watch.

"Ready, darling?" Max asked, leaning back into the interior of the limousine, his tawny hair falling forward over his forehead, making him look like a young king ready to mount his snow-white charger and ride off to do battle with the dragon. "Hey, hon, smile! Don't you remember? I already promised—everything is going to be just fine."

"Max the giant killer—oh, yes, I remember. Now all you have to do is tell everyone else." Extending her hand, Julia allowed her husband to help her from the limousine.

"Max, are you sure you don't want any?" Margaret Sutherland asked, a pink plastic scoop poised over the open half gallon of fudge-ripple ice cream. "Now that we know Jim is going to be fine, we're allowed to reward ourselves a bit and celebrate, and sundaes are a Sutherland family tradition."

Max smiled and shook his head, reaching for the steaming cup of coffee that Julia had placed before him a few moments earlier.

Julia looked at her husband. They had stayed at the hospital until the end of visiting hours and then Max had treated the women to dinner at a local restaurant. It was nearly ten o'clock and she was sure the last thing on Max's mind was dessert. He was more interested in learning the sleeping arrangements Margaret had made for the night. She hid a grin. Actually, when she thought about it, maybe "dessert" was very much on the man's mind. What a pity—for Max.

"Oh, go ahead, Max," Julia chided, heading for the refrigerator and the can of whipped cream her mother had told her was inside it. She agreed with her mother; they did have cause for celebration. As a matter of fact, she herself was feeling almost giddy with relief. "Women hate to make gluttons of themselves unless they can fatten everybody else up in the process."

"And where do you hide your fat, Julia, in your earlobes?" Max asked, seemingly oblivious to the fact that his wife was now standing behind him, the cap off the whipped cream, and the nozzle pointed directly at the top of his head.

Wouldn't he look lovely with a fluffy white pouf crown? she thought, wondering if it was possible to become drunk on happiness. She rolled her eyes mischievously, reluctantly resisting temptation. "Oh,

Max," she said, sitting down beside him. "You don't know how lucky you are. Mother, I'll take two scoops, please, and some fudge, if you have it."

Julia was euphoric, liberated, at peace with the world and in love with it at the same time. Her father was going to be just fine! His ailment was common enough, the doctors had told Max and her, especially in this laid-back, retiree-oriented community. Jim Sutherland, who had worked hard all his life was, as one young intern had summed it up, "bored out of his skull."

How boredom had turned into a mild depression, and that mild depression into real organic symptoms was still not totally clear to Julia. It was enough to know that her father's heart was fine, and all he really needed was to feel useful once again. Margaret had passed over this diagnosis as nonsense, concentrating on Jim's dangerously high cholesterol level.

Margaret placed a bowl of ice cream covered in hot fudge in front of her daughter and Julia proceeded to cover it from rim to rim in a swirling avalanche of whipped cream.

"What, no cherry on top?" Max asked, looking down at the overloaded bowl in what seemed to be considerable awe. "What's the matter, hon, are you afraid of overdoing it?"

Julia ignored him, concentrating instead on the pure sensual pleasure of cold ice cream, warm fudge and airy whipped cream as they melted against the inside of her mouth. Her eyes closed, she gloried in the mingled tastes and textures, knowing she was driving Max silently crazy with the rapturous expression on her face. She knew, because he had seen her eat a sundae before and had told her so. Giving in to temptation, she flicked out the tip of her tongue, capturing a random fleck of whipped cream that clung to her upper lip.

"God, Julia, would you please knock that off," Max groaned quietly, so that Margaret, who was putting away the ice cream, didn't hear him.

Keeping her head straight, Julia shifted her eyes to the left to look at Max. Oh, yes, he was dying inside—absolutely *dying*—and it served him right! She took a second spoonful of the sundae, lingering over it a moment before slowly withdrawing the spoon from her mouth, still looking at him. "What's the matter, Max?" she drawled sweetly. "Are you missing your little candy striper?"

"Sheila?" Max hissed, leaning toward her. "Is that what this is all about? You can't be serious, Julia. The kid's no more than sixteen. I was only being polite."

Julia's eyelids came down to hide her expression. "Of course you were, Max. It isn't your fault that the poor girl is starting a Max Rafferty fan club."

"You're jealous!" Max exploded, causing Margaret to look at her daughter.

"Keep your voice down, and don't flatter yourself," Julia warned, smiling at her mother. "Didn't Dad ask one of us to call him before ten, Mother? Are you tired, or do you want to do it?"

Margaret sat down at the round table, her ice cream in front of her. "I'll do it, pet, but not until I've had my ice cream. You heard the doctor say that Dad's cholesterol level is high, and I wouldn't want him to know I'm eating something he can't have. Poor baby, he loves his sweets so much. Now, why are you jealous, Julia?''

''She's jealous because she thinks a little girl at the hospital flirted with me,'' Max said, smiling at his mother-in-law. ''Tell her, Margaret—I can't help it if I'm irresistible, can I?''

Julia stood up. ''Oh, brother. Excuse me, Mother, while I get a cup of coffee to help me wash down that bilge. The man attracts women to him like velvet attracts lint, and then he has the nerve to blame the lint!''

Margaret laughed, reaching across the table to take Max's hand. ''Oh, Max, it's so good to have you here. It's even good to hear the two of you squabbling— especially since I know you're back together again. Julia, you know Max can't help it. He's just naturally attractive to women. He'd never betray your trust in him. He loves you dearly, sweetheart. Isn't that right, Max?''

Julia turned away from the stove just in time to look into Max's eyes. His beautiful, blue ''trust me'' eyes. ''I love her with all my heart, Margaret,'' he said slowly, ''and I'd rather walk out of her life again tomorrow than hurt a single hair on her head.'' He lifted Margaret's hand to his mouth and kissed it, his eyes still on Julia. ''You have my word on it.''

Margaret took back her hand, bringing it to her cheek. ''Oh, Julia, I don't know how you let this man get away the first time. Your father was never so romantic, much as I love him. Max has even bought you a new engagement ring, just as if you're courting again. Your father, bless him, thinks he has done me a huge favor if he buys me a new self-propelled vacuum cleaner for our anniversary."

Julia quickly placed the full coffee cup on the table before her shaking hands betrayed her sudden nervousness. How could she have forgotten about Luke's ring? She knew how observant her mother was. Thank heaven she had planned to bring Luke with her on her next trip to Florida, as a sort of surprise, and hadn't told her parents about her engagement. "Um, yes, the ring is new, Mother," she stammered at last, looking to Max for help.

Margaret took one last bite of ice cream. "Well, I think it's perfectly lovely, but I imagine, Julia, you'll want to go down to the bank with me tomorrow morning anyway."

Julia was confused, and she didn't like the way Max was looking at her. "The bank?"

Rising to take her dish to the sink, Margaret said, "Yes, dear, the bank. Don't you remember? Dad put your wedding and engagement rings in our safe deposit box for you. I know you wanted to send them back to Max—after we talked you out of throwing them in the ocean—but now I'm glad we kept them for you. Your father always knew you'd need them again one day. Max, did you see how happy Jim was when you two came into his room together?"

Max leaned forward to answer Margaret's last question, and the two of them began discussing the doctor's diagnosis of a mixture of stress and mild depression while Julia sat back, her left thumb stroking the thin gold band of Luke's ring.

Her mind felt as light and airy—and useless—as the empty calories in whipped cream. What was she going to do? She certainly wasn't going to take off Luke's ring, to replace it with the wide gold band and gigantic diamond she had taken from her hand nearly five year earlier.

She was engaged to Luke Manning now, even if her marriage to Max was still technically in effect. She had to put a stop to this farce, this insane masquerade, and she had to do it immediately. Her father wasn't in any real danger. He was an intelligent man, capable of hearing the truth. She couldn't let her parents build castles in the air over this supposed reconciliation for another moment!

Convinced she was right, Julia leaned forward to interrupt her mother and Max, only to hear Max say, "And so, Margaret, when my lawyer told me the divorce Julia got on impulse in some South American country was invalid, I raced to Allentown to reclaim my wife. We'd only been together for two days when you called, and the rest, as they say, just happened."

Julia's mouth dropped open. Her mother was dabbing at the corners of her eyes with her napkin, clearly overcome by Max's ridiculous half truths. Julia turned to glare at Max, willing him to self-destruct, when the telephone rang in the hall and her mother ran to answer it, saying she was sure it was Jim, who must have gotten tired of waiting for a call.

"Uh-oh," Max said, raising his eyebrows. "There's that cold, silent black stare again, boring all the way into my brain. Surprise, hon, but it just doesn't scare me anymore. As a matter of fact, I'm beginning to like it. It means I'm getting to you, doesn't it, sweet-heart?"

"I detest you," Julia muttered, reaching for the dish of half-melted sundae, then abandoning the idea. This was her mother's house, and she wouldn't make a scene. Besides, she'd have to clean it all up later, and chocolate fudge could be a real pain. "How could you lie to my mother like that?"

Max shrugged, getting up to walk out onto the lanai. "How could I not, hon? We agreed to keep up a front while your father is in the hospital. It's only for a few more days. Besides, I didn't lie. I just didn't tell all of the truth."

"There's a difference?" Julia spat angrily, jump-ing up to follow him outside into the darkness. "I should have gotten you with the whipped cream when I had the chance."

Max stopped, turning to face her. "You mean when you were getting the container out of the refrigera-tor?" he asked, surprising her. "I agree, it was a golden opportunity, but it's too late now. Always act on your impulses, hon, then you never have anything to regret. For instance, right now I have this over-whelming impulse to kiss you."

"You wouldn't!" Julia exclaimed just before Max's arms gripped her hard at the shoulders and he hauled her up against his hard body, his mouth crushed against hers.

All the worry she had felt for her father, all the twisted, tortured feelings she had been experiencing since Max had come charging back into her life to complicate it, all the lost sleep and stress and half-buried longings exploded at once into a powerful mushroom cloud of passion as Julia responded to Max's kiss.

Her arms flew around him, her fingers clawing at his back as she fought to hold him closer. Her mouth opened, drawing him in, her tongue dueling with his for possession. Her body moved against his hungrily, aching for—

"No!" She pulled away, taking several deep breaths as she struggled for control. "No, Max, not this time," she said at last, her pulses racing, but her strong will firmly back under control. "Love doesn't begin like this. It begins in the mind, in the heart. Love isn't presents, or possession, or bodies groping together in the dark. Love is respect, and consideration for the other person's personal freedom, and—and—"

"And wanting to bear his name, and his children, and accepting his need to care for her...to protect her from all harm...to cherish her because she's more important to him than the very air he breathes," Max concluded quietly before turning to walk out into the dew-damp yard and disappear into the darkness.

Julia leaned against a post supporting the lanai roof, thankful it was there or else she may have fallen. "Oh, God, Max," she whispered brokenly once he was gone, a hand to her lips, "you just don't play fair."

Chapter Nine

Julia counted each separate ring of the telephone on Luke's private line, not sure if she wanted him to pick up or not. What was she going to say to him? She certainly couldn't tell him that she and Max had shared the same room last night, the same king-size bed.

Nothing had happened, of course. Max had been too occupied sulking to come into the bedroom until after midnight, which was when she had at last fallen into an exhausted sleep. And if she had awoken this morning with her arm around his back, well, she could explain that easily enough. It had become chilly during the night, and she had instinctively reached out for warmth. Wellington hadn't been there to warm her feet, and she had used Max as a substitute. She had realized her error at once and beat a hasty retreat to the bathroom before Max could wake up and try to turn her innocent mistake to his advantage.

No, she couldn't tell Luke any of that. He wouldn't believe it. She didn't even believe it, and she had been there.

Damn Max Rafferty! she thought angrily, and damn these rings I'm wearing! Looking down at her left hand, she saw the wide gold band of possession and the large solitaire nestled beside it. Her right hand, the one clutching the receiver in a death grip, held Luke's marquise ring.

She looked, or so Julia thought, like a little girl playing dress-up with her mother's jewelry. It just didn't seem right to wear so many diamonds in Florida, in the middle of the day, with cotton slacks, a loose plaid jacket and a tank top. And, she added silently, looking toward the floor, bare feet.

"Hello. Dr. Manning here."

Luke's deep voice took her by surprise, and she had to physically shake herself back to awareness. "Luke, it's Julia!"

"Darling! I tried phoning you this morning but your mother said you were sleeping in. Actually," she heard him say, his voice only slightly strained, "she said you and Max were sleeping in."

"Yes," Julia answered quickly, "we were both tired from the flight, I guess. Luke, Dad's much better. The doctors down here say the whole episode is stress related."

"I've already heard, darling. Your mother told me all about it, although I don't think your mother believes it yet. I guess not everyone was built for retirement. I know I'd go crazy if I couldn't work. When will you be coming home? I miss you."

Julia was barely listening. Max was standing behind her. She could feel his presence, smell his subtle
after-shave, even though she couldn't see him. "I miss
you too, darling," she said distinctly, stiffening her
spine—and her resolve—as Max's fingertips slid up
the side of her throat, to begin playing at her left ear.
"I miss you *terribly.*"

"Liar," Max whispered in her ear, his warm breath
doing strange things to her equilibrium. "You weren't
missing him last night, Mrs. Rafferty, while you were
snuggling up to me."

"Julia? Is someone there with you?"

"Is someone here with me?" She reached up to grab
Max's tie, pulling him down so that his face was at eye
level with hers. "No, darling, or at least no one *important,*" she said, her teeth gritted.

Max puckered up his mouth and made kissing
sounds with his lips until Julia let go of his tie and
pushed him away. "What did you say, darling?" she
asked Luke. "Um, Mother just came in with some
groceries and I couldn't hear you."

"Good save," Max complimented, saluting her
quick recovery. He sat down cross-legged on the floor
in front of her, his chin in his hands. "Now tell him
about the rings."

"Shut up!"

"What?" Luke's voice came to her through the
telephone.

"No—no, Luke, darling, I didn't mean you," Julia hastened into speech, shaking a fist at Max.
"Mother's dog is barking."

"Your parents don't have a dog, sweetheart," Max corrected silkily. "Careful, love of my life, or your nose will begin to grow. Such a pity, and I'm so attracted to that little nose."

Julia covered the mouthpiece with her hand. "You're just loving this, aren't you, Max? I think you're sick!"

Max rolled onto his back, his legs in the air, reminding Julia of Wellington when he wanted a treat. "Yes, yes," he said, looking up at her piteously. "I'm sick, I'm dying—I need mouth-to-mouth resuscitation. Help me, Julia!"

"Luke," Julia said at last, turning on the chair so that her back was to Max and his bad canine imitation, "I have to go now. I'll phone you again later."

"It's Max, isn't it?" Luke asked, and Julia rolled her eyes, knowing that, although Luke was intelligent, it wouldn't have taken a nuclear physicist to figure out that Max Rafferty's fine hand was running havoc through this conversation. "He's making good use of this time with you, isn't he? I know I would if I had the chance."

Julia looked up as Max walked past her, into the kitchen, without looking back. Obviously he was done playing the fool, now that he had succeeded in driving any thoughts of a romantic conversation with Luke out of her head. "He has his moments, Luke," she admitted, sighing, "but I think he's going to let us alone now. Tell me, how's that patient you had to operate on Sunday afternoon?"

* * *

It was late when they finally got to bed that night, Max having agreed to Margaret's suggestion that the three of them play Scrabble after returning from the hospital.

He won, of course. Max always won, except when he allowed someone else to win, which was something he rarely did with Julia, for she always seemed to know when he was trying to lose.

He was in bed before she finished washing her face, so that she stood in the bathroom doorway for a moment, mentally measuring the distance between herself and the bed before turning out the bathroom light.

Max turned his head slightly, to see how clearly Julia's body was outlined against the sheer cotton of her simple, floor-length gown. The small light was revealing more than she realized, and he didn't tell her. He only laid there, his hands balling into fists, his stomach muscles tautening with desire.

The light went out at last and he heard rather than saw Julia making her way to the bed. Holding his breath, he waited for her to slide under the sheet, keeping as much of the bed between them as humanly possible without falling onto the floor.

They laid quietly for a long time, with only the sound of the overhead fan audible in the room, until Max was sure Julia was quivering with tension—and then he made his move. He was subtle, yawning widely, then turning onto his side, positioning himself closer to her by at least two highly encouraging feet.

Julia didn't move. She stayed on her back, her eyes open, staring up at the ceiling fan that was barely visible in the slight moonlight filtering in through the venetian blinds.

Ten minutes passed, then fifteen.

Max moved again, rolling onto his back, his right foot becoming temporarily imprisoned by the sheet before he could accomplish his latest maneuver.

He was beside her now, no more than half a foot away, and closing fast.

She still hadn't reacted; hadn't made a single move to either acknowledge him or push him away; hadn't sat up and accused him of trying to do what he was, in actuality, trying his damnedest to do.

Max counted to one hundred very slowly, at least until he got to eighty. From there, he counted by twos. And then he groaned, as if dreaming, and turned onto his side, his right thigh connecting with the side of her leg.

"Max?" Julia's voice was a low caress.

"Um?" he answered drowsily, nearly purring.

"Are you comfortable, darling?" Julia asked sweetly, sending Max's burgeoning hopes into the stratosphere.

He snugged closer. "Uh-huh."

"That's good, darling. There's only one little thing..."

"Hmm?" He could have said more, but he didn't think it was time to be articulate. Through the ages, man had gotten much further by keeping his mouth shut and his senses alert.

"My left arm is uncomfortable," Julia complained, sighing.

"Ahh," he commiserated, moving his leg slightly, feeling her gown begin to ride up at least three heartening inches.

"You see, Max, it hurts because I've stretched it out toward the nightstand so that I can hold on to this glass of cold water that I'm about to pour on your head unless you get back on your side of the bed in the next five seconds. One...two..."

"Julia, darling, you wouldn't."

"Your leg, Max," she warned tightly. "Move it or lose it. And then move the rest of you. I'm still counting—three...four..."

"Goodnight, Julia," Max said shortly, moving back to his side of the bed.

"Goodnight, Max," Julia answered, silently congratulating herself for her brilliance, while at the same time knowing that all the raging water walled up behind Hoover Dam wouldn't have kept Max away if he'd really wanted her.

That disheartening thought kept her awake long after Max's soft, even breathing told her he was fast asleep.

Julia lingered in the bedroom long after Max had showered, dressed and joined Margaret in the kitchen. She had opted to stay home this morning, and Max had volunteered to drive her mother to the hospital before coming back to the house so that he could make some business calls to New York.

She made the bed, then emptied the glass of water she had used to preserve her "chastity" against her own husband, before sitting down in the pink-and-green chintz chaise longue, her feet tucked up inside her white dressing gown.

She was miserable. There was no nice word to use, no sweet, mind-soothing euphemism such as "fatigued" or "out of sorts" or even "a trifle depressed." No, she was miserable—knocked down, dragged out, go out in the garden and eat worms miserable—and it was all Max's fault!

How could he do this to her? How could he come waltzing back into her life now, just when she thought she had gotten it all together? She was going to marry Luke. Luke was a wonderful man, a caring man, a passionate man—or at least he showed every sign of being passionate.

So why hadn't she gone to bed with Luke? It wasn't as if she were still some unschooled virgin, waiting to give herself to her husband on her wedding night. She had done that once, and look where that had gotten her, for crying out loud!

Yet she had asked Luke to wait, and he had respected her wishes. Ha! she thought, making the face her mother had told her years ago never to make, for it made her look like an angry Pekingese. *And I'll just bet Max took a vow of chastity the whole time we were apart! Oh, yeah, sure he did—and the moon really is made of green cheese!*

She snuggled against the overstuffed pillows. She wouldn't think about Max's possible romantic exploits while they were apart. It upset her, and she didn't want to be upset about the idea of Max being with another woman, no matter how casually men might look at such situations. It didn't feel casual to her.

Actually, it shouldn't feel one way or the other to her. It was none of her business what Max had done while they had been apart. There it was again—she kept thinking in terms of "when they had been apart." They still *were* apart! They weren't back together, no matter how much Max wanted to pretend that they were. And they weren't going to be together, not now, not ever again.

She didn't want him, for one thing. She had Luke now, and Luke was who she wanted. Did Max really think a scrap of paper was going to make any difference? A divorce decree meant nothing. They were incompatible, totally and completely incompatible.

"He was wonderful with Mother and Dad," she said aloud, shifting uncomfortably on the chaise longue. "And he handled everything beautifully at home when he got the call, and ever since we got here. Max has always been wonderful at handling things."

She bit her lip. "Just the way he wanted to handle me when I told him about Sutherland. I could see the gleam in his eye. He didn't want me to have Sutherland unless he had his fingerprints all over it, controlling me and every move I made. He wants to protect me, he says. He wants to cherish me. Wrong! He just wants to be in charge. Well, I can take care of myself!"

She turned onto her side and spied a paperback book on the table beside the chaise longue. It looked familiar, and she picked it up. "Good Lord, it's Holly's astrology book. Now where did that come from?"

She gingerly opened the book, scanning the table of contents. "Here it is, Leo." She turned to the first page of the chapter devoted to Leo the Lion, the supposed king of the zodiac.

"Leo, a fire sign—fixed, whatever that means—a positive force ruled by the sun. Symbol, the lion. Yeah, well, what else would it be, a duck-billed platypus? Careful, Scorpio, you're being sarcastic," she warned herself wryly, once more scrunching her features into that of an angry Pekingese.

"Virtues—loyalty, affection, vitality, good looks, wonderful organizer, self-confident. Well, they have that right at least. Not-so-great characteristics—arrogance, tyrannical nature, vanity, angers easily, egotism. Lord, the author must know Max personally! Famous Leos—Napoleon Bonaparte and Lucille Ball." She laughed out loud. "Bonaparte *and* Lucy? I should have guessed!"

Snuggling down against the cushions, Julia turned the page and began to read all about her husband.

Chapter Ten

Max lay back in the canvas lawn chair, stretching lazily as the late-afternoon sun warmed his skin. Dark sunglasses hid his blue eyes as he gazed across the backyard, idly watching a large orange-striped cat stalk a yellow-and-black butterfly poised on the tip of a long blade of grass.

The cat sat motionless in the grass, its chin parallel with its outstretched neck, hunkered down on its haunches, while its slowly undulating rump and fat tail pointed toward the sky. The animal didn't blink, it didn't move, and Max looked hard, trying to see if the cat was even breathing.

He transferred his attention to the butterfly, still delicately perched atop the blade of grass, its decorative wings opening and closing slowly, as if the exotic insect was fanning itself. It seemed oblivious, or icily indifferent, to any danger.

Max sat forward, intrigued, and tried to decide whether he should be rooting for the orange cat or the exotic butterfly. Both were beautiful, sleek and graceful.

But there was something especially fascinating about the orange cat. He seemed to rule his kingdom, even though it was nothing more than a suburban backyard, and he very definitely resented this confident intruder, no matter how she—Max found himself thinking of the butterfly as a she—graced his kingdom with her sophisticated beauty.

The cat began to move forward, slowly, each carefully placed paw advancing him toward his potential victim. Max swallowed hard, waiting for the cat to launch himself into the air, capture the pretty insect in his jaws and devour it.

It never happened; the destruction that had seemed inevitable never came. The cat stopped a full two feet away from the butterfly, his left front paw suspended in midair, and raised his head, effectively calling off the hunt. He laid down in the grass, rolled slowly onto his side and began grooming himself in a patch of sunlight that filtered through the trees, while the butterfly continued to fan herself.

Both exotic creatures now occupied their own space in the backyard, each gracing it with their own individual beauty, each adding something special to the scene—and neither was threatened, neither was superior to the other.

The butterfly knew she could fly away at any time, and the cat knew he could capture the butterfly, but neither made the move. They had, at least for the moment, learned to coexist. They might even learn to like and respect each other, if they just gave it a chance.

Max leaned back against the canvas chair, a sinking feeling invading his stomach. "If I were a profound person, I'd say there was a lesson in this for me," he said aloud, so that the cat stopped grooming himself to glare at him challengingly.

Rising, Max addressed the cat, knowing he was being silly, but not really caring. "You think you're hot stuff, don't you, fella? Well, let me tell you, you leave Jul—...that butterfly alone. You may be king here, but she's the queen, and you wouldn't look half so good without her!"

"Max? Is someone out there with you?"

Max turned around to see Jim Sutherland coming toward him from the kitchen. He wasn't embarrassed to have been caught talking to an animal, because Max didn't embarrass easily. "What? No, nobody's here. I was just discussing life with that cat over there. I think he believes we're the trespassers in his kingdom, and not the other way around. Did you have a nice nap, Jim? The ladies should be back from the store soon. Margaret promised us something special for dinner your first night home."

Jim Sutherland sat his long, lean body in a nearby canvas chair, pulling a face. "If it has anything to do with ground turkey, oat bran or yogurt, I may file for divorce. God, Max, what I wouldn't do for a two-inch thick, juicy steak—rare—and smothered in pork chops. And baked potatoes with sour cream—they'd be good, too."

Max looked at his father-in-law, whose long bones, great posture and dark mahogany hair Julia had inherited to such advantage. Jim and Julia were such contrasts to the rather short, pudgy Margaret, who had been tinting her hair blonde ever since, according to her, she had first seen signs of gray thirty years previously. "Don't forget dessert, Jim," he pointed out, retaking his own seat on the other chair. "There's always a chance you might get lucky there, right?"

"Dessert?" Jim sniffed, rolling his eyes. "If you're talking about sugarfree gelatin with pineapple slices, you can just forget it." He leaned forward, looking about as if checking for spies. "Max, there's this ice cream parlor about five blocks down the street. It just opened last week and I don't think Margaret has gotten wind of it yet. They make a banana split that could tempt a man to give up sex, it's that good. Do you think—"

Max shook his head. "First of all, Jim, nothing's *that* good," he joked, laughing. "And, secondly, it would be worth my life to sneak behind Margaret's back that way. She and Julia shopped all day yesterday, filling this house from one end to the other with cholesterol-free, low-fat foods. She tried one of the recipes on me last night. I didn't know they could make meatloaf with carrots and ground turkey."

Jim dropped his forehead into his hands, showing all the signs of a thoroughly beaten man. "Oh, Lord, Max, maybe I should have kept my mouth shut when my chest started to hurt. Look at me. My heart is fine! Why is she doing this to me?"

Max poured two glasses of sugar-free lemonade from the thermos Julia had placed on the lanai earlier, and handed one to Jim. "Margaret is doing this, my friend, because she loves you very much and she doesn't want your cholesterol level to climb higher than the national debt. Besides, for some reason, wives seem to think it's their fault if their men aren't healthy, and they get all guilty about it."

"Why? She doesn't put the fork in my hand, for Pete's sake." Jim stood up, his hands deep in the pants of his light blue golfing slacks, and stared out into the backyard. "God, Max, but I hate it here. If this is paradise, I'll take vanilla."

Max looked up at his father-in-law in surprise. The man didn't make sense. "Then why are you here?" he asked, for Max would never remain anyplace if he didn't want to be there. "I don't see any chain around your ankle."

"Simple. Margaret loves it here," Jim replied, a muscle beginning to work in his cheek. "I was offered early retirement when the plant closed up shop in Allentown and relocated to South Carolina. Margaret was all for taking it. She said I had worked hard all my life and deserved some time in the sun. Ha! Do you know what it's like to play golf six days a week with a bunch of old men?" He turned to look at Max. "It's terrible! Almost as terrible as playing canasta every other evening at the senior center. I don't feel old, Max, so why do I feel so damn useless?"

Oh boy, Max thought, shifting in his seat. So this was the depression the doctors had warned them about the day he and Julia had arrived. "Does Margaret know how you feel?'' he questioned, wondering if it was wise to get involved in what could prove to be a ticklish situation.

Jim shook his head. "It would break her heart, Max. Margaret loves it here. After we loaned Julia the money to start her business and moved down here—well, I guess this leisure business is something a person has to get used to sooner or later. Let me tell you, Max, it isn't easy.''

His father-in-law could have told him that his hair was on fire and it wouldn't have mattered, because Max wasn't listening anymore. Had he heard the man correctly? Jim and Margaret had loaned Julia the money to start Sutherland? Jim and Margaret had loaned his *wife* the money to start her business?

How could she have done this to him? How dare she go to someone else—even if it was family—rather than him, her own husband? And she told him she had wanted to be independent! Max's hands balled into fists. He wanted to hit something. He wanted to scream. He wanted to grab Julia by her slim white shoulders and shake her until her teeth rattled!

"Max?''

Max looked up, seeing Jim through a red haze of rage. "What?'' he asked hotly, then quickly controlled himself. "I'm sorry, Jim. I must have been daydreaming there for a moment. Did you say you and Margaret loaned Julia the money for Sutherland?''

Jim smiled, shaking his head. "We wanted to give it to her outright, but Julia wouldn't have any part of it. She paid it all back, too, with interest. She's quite a girl, our Julia.''

"Quite a girl?" Max muttered under his breath. "You bet your sweet—"

"Hi! We thought you two men might be out here," Margaret Sutherland said cheerfully, interrupting Max just as he was about to launch himself into the upper atmosphere on the full head of steam he was building up inside his skull.

Margaret crossed the lanai to stand up on tiptoe and kiss her husband's cheek. "Are you hungry yet, dear? Julia and I found some nice lean veal at the market. I'm going to make my own oatmeal bread crumbs for veal cutlet, and we'll have a huge salad of greens to go along with it. We also found a low-calorie salad dressing that comes in a spray bottle, so that you can't overdo it. Doesn't that sound lovely?"

"That sounds delicious, dear," Jim answered, slipping his arm around his wife's shoulders. "Or maybe I can skip the salad and just come back out here and graze."

"What?" Margaret asked, looking up at her husband. "Oh, you're making a joke, aren't you? Max, isn't Jim funny?"

"He's a real riot, Margaret." Max counted to ten, deliberately damping down his anger. "Margaret, is Julia inside?" he asked carelessly, just as Jim opened his mouth, undoubtedly to tell his wife that he hadn't really tried to be amusing.

Margaret turned to look at her son-in-law. "Yes, dear, she is. I believe she said something about having a quick bath before dinner."

Max excused himself, his hands still drawn up into fists, and stomped toward the house, stopping only long enough to ask Jim if he knew whether or not cats responded to commands.

"Commands, Max? What sort of commands do you mean?" Jim asked.

"Like *sic 'em!*" Max spat, turning on his heels once more.

"Aaahhh." Julia slid into the warm water, allowing the thick layer of lightly perfumed bubbles to close over her body, nearly covering her up to the chin. She had always loved bubble baths, but rarely found time for them anymore.

When she had spied the bottle of bubble bath at the store while shopping with her mother, Julia had succumbed to temptation, hoping a long soak in the tub would ease away some of the muscle aches caused by her tension-inducing sleeping arrangements with Max.

Three nights spent hanging on to the edge of the mattress for dear life was not exactly Julia's idea of rest, and she couldn't wait for this last night to be over so that she could return to her own bed, in her own house—safely back in her own world—while Max continued on to New York.

She was sure he couldn't stay away from Majestic Enterprises much longer—any more than she could remain out of touch with Sutherland for another day—no matter how good his vice presidents were at running the show in his absence. Max was a hands-on executive by nature, and she couldn't believe he enjoyed sitting back while other people did his work for him.

The book said that about him too, Julia remembered, smiling as she picked up the soap and began lathering her shoulders. Actually, the book had said quite a lot about Max, and most of it had been eerily correct. It had mentioned his quick temper, his sulks, his gifts and even his inability to ever admit he was wrong or apologize. Of course, it had also been completely off base in some ways as well.

Max, according to the book, could feel very insecure and needed to be reassured that he was all right. That, of course, was utter nonsense. Maximillian Rafferty didn't have an insecure bone in his entire, magnificent body. There was no room for one among all that arrogance and egotism!

Julia held the bar of soap between her hands, rotating it slowly as she watched her movements form bubbles that squeezed between her fingers, covering the backs of her hands—and her odd assortment of engagement rings—like strange, translucent pearls. If only Max did need her.

But Max had never needed her, or anyone. He was an entity entirely unto himself, a totally unique individual who radiated the fact that he was superior to everyone else in the world and made no apologies for that fact. If he let someone into his realm it was only because he was feeling generous, or because he felt they added something to his consequence.

He didn't need her—he wanted her. He liked the way she looked beside him. She complimented him, which was a long way from complementing him!

Her biggest mistake had been letting him see how much she had adored him. If she had been willing to go through life as nothing more than his adoring handmaiden, content to bask in the reflected glow of his magnificence, they would most probably still be together. But Julia had needed more from life than that, and she had needed more from Max than he had seemed willing to give.

Thinking about Max and his supposed Leo traits was giving Julia a headache. She leaned back against the soft sponge cushion she had placed behind her head, purposefully clearing her mind, content to daydream while the warm water and bubble bath did its work on her slowly relaxing body.

The door to the bathroom opened so quickly that its movement sent a small breeze dancing over the bubbles, threatening to scatter them. A heartbeat later the wooden door crashed against the wall and Max was standing inside the steamy bathroom, his handsome face nearly purple with rage.

Julia, startled, began to sit up, then thought better of it and sank even lower beneath the bubbles, her features setting themselves into a haughty, expressionless mask. "I should have known this would happen when I noticed that the lock was broken. What do you want, Max?"

"What do I want?" he bellowed without preamble. "Oh, you're good, Julia, I'll have to give you that. You're so cool, so together. Nothing upsets you, nothing can break through that ice-maiden exterior—until you start throwing things, that is. Well, I'll tell you what I want, Ms. Sutherland. I want you to explain to me why you borrowed money from your parents to start Sutherland—*that's* what the hell I want to know!''

Julia's eyes widened momentarily, as Max had taken her completely by surprise. "I see," she responded slowly, wishing she were dressed and in an upright position. She felt entirely too vulnerable like this, her hair tied up haphazardly on top of her head, lying naked beneath a thin layer of rapidly disappearing bubbles. "And what business would that be of yours, Max? We weren't married anymore."

Max took two steps toward the tub. "Wrong! The hell we weren't, lady! You were going into business and you went to your parents for money rather than come to me—and I want to know why. What was the matter, Julia? Didn't you think I'd give it to you?"

Julia felt her muscles begin to tighten. "Oh, yes, Max, I knew you'd give it to me—with *give* being the operative word. First you'd give me the money, and then you'd take over my business. Sutherland would have been my little toy, a little fish you would have flipped your wife to keep her happy when you couldn't have her in bed, keeping her happy there. Well, no thank you, Max. I didn't want any part of it!"

Max ran a hand through his hair, pacing up and down the length of the small bathroom as if he would explode at any moment.

"Is that what you thought, Julia—what you still think? That I treated you like a toy? And how did you treat our marriage? You wouldn't even use my name, for crying out loud. Sutherland! Your business should have been Rafferty or *Julia*—anything but Sutherland! Don't you know what an insult that was, Julia? My God, I can't believe this!''

Julia looked across the room to where her white dressing gown was hanging on a hook beside the shower stall, silently measuring her chances of getting out of the tub and grabbing it before Max's passionate anger could convert itself to pure passion.

She decided not to risk it.

''Of course you can't believe it, Max,'' she said as he continued to pace. ''You can't believe it because you never take the time to listen to anyone but yourself. That last night wasn't the first time I had tried to talk to you about my business plans, but you didn't want to hear them. I'd say one word and you'd be off, telling me how we would take the fashion world by storm. With my style and your business brain—and that's exactly what you said, Max—there would be no stopping us.''

Max stopped pacing to glare at her. ''And what's so wrong with that?'' he bellowed, clearly unable to see any error in his plan.

Julia sadly shook her head. ''Oh, Max, never mind. It's too late now to go back over it. Tell you what—I was wrong, you were right. You're *always* right. The great Maximillian Rafferty is never wrong about anything, just ask him! Only it's still over. Sutherland belongs to me, and you have Majestic Enterprises. It seems fair enough.''

Max leaned forward, looking down at her in the tub. ''Damn it, don't patronize me, Julia, because I'm not in the mood!'' he warned tightly.

No, he wasn't in the mood. Julia could see that very clearly. She also knew that she was on the verge of losing her temper, and if the two of them really began going at it her parents were sure to hear them. Somehow, some way, she had to get them out of this ticklish situation before Max broke a blood vessel or she smacked him with the sopping sponge.

Suddenly, as if inspired, Julia remembered something from the astrology book. If she was smart, the book had said, she could deflect a Leo's temper by the simple means of giving him a compliment. Leos loved to be complimented, as long as it was a genuine compliment, and it soothed the savage beast better than anything else.

She felt guilty, and even a little silly, but she also realized that she had nothing to lose by trying it. Looking at him, and noticing the slight tan he had gotten in the three days they had been in Florida, she said earnestly, "You know, Max, for all the trouble you've had to put up with by helping me with Mother and Dad—and I really appreciate how you've helped us—it hasn't been all bad for you. Florida seems to agree with you. You really look good with that tan."

She leaned back, warily waiting for him to tell her she was crazy, that he looked like hell because his wife was driving him into early old age! It didn't happen.

Max stepped back, lifted a hand to his cheek, and smiled. "You think so?" he asked, looking down at her. "You know how I feel about Margaret and Jim. But thank you, Julia, thank you very much."

"You—you're welcome," she answered automatically, not quite believing her own ears. It was insane!

Max's anger had been shut off as quickly as she was accustomed to seeing it turned on, and he seemed close to purring with sudden contentment.

"Max," she began, hoping to press this slight advantage, "would you mind stepping outside a moment so that I can get out of the tub now? I'm beginning to feel cold."

Max's smiling blue eyes narrowed perceptively as he ran his gaze down the length of her body. The book hadn't warned her about this. Having his sunny good humor back was a godsend, but she wasn't sure if she needed his amorous glances.

"Max?" she asked tremulously, sinking farther into the bathtub.

"Julia?" he answered silkily, beginning to open his shirt as he stepped out of his loafers.

She shook her head. "No, Max," she warned, holding out one hand to stop him as his hands went to his belt buckle.

"Why not, darling?" he countered, turning to close the bathroom door. "It may not be as big as the bathtub in Vermont, but I think we can manage it."

"Oh, Max," Julia groaned, close to tears. "You know we can't. It would just complicate things, and they're already complicated enough as it is." She looked down to see that the bubbles had all but disappeared. "Please, Max, don't do this."

His slacks slipped to the floor and Julia sat, transfixed, looking at Max's magnificent body. She knew every inch of it, had loved every inch of it, and she felt her head begin to swim as she longed to succumb to the ecstasy Max was offering her.

"Max—" she began, just as a knock sounded on the bathroom door.

"Julia, dinner's almost ready," she heard her mother call through the closed door. "Do you know where Max has disappeared to, dear? We can't seem to find him anywhere, which worries me, because he seemed a little upset earlier."

As Max opened his mouth to speak, Julia answered hastily, daring him with her eyes to contradict her. "He went for a walk, Mother." Throwing caution to the wind, she then stood up, hopped out of the tub and grabbed the dressing gown before Max could do more than grin his appreciation.

Giving him a look that would have welded a lesser man to the tile floor, she pushed him into the shower stall, kicked his shirt and slacks in after him, and opened the door to the bedroom.

"Ah, Mother!" she said brightly, closing the door behind her and leaning against it as she struggled to keep the dressing gown from clinging to her wet, soapy legs. "It sure does smell good out here. Is that the veal? Have you set the table yet? Don't worry, I can do that for you."

"Julia," her mother said disapprovingly, looking down, "you're dripping all over the carpet. Dinner isn't ready yet. There's no reason to be in such a rush. Take your time, dear, and dry off carefully before you get dressed."

"Yes, Mother," Julia agreed sheepishly, stepping away from the door, feeling childish and foolish as Margaret left the bedroom, yet knowing she also felt infinitely safer than she had just a few short minutes ago.

"Dry your back, lady?" Max questioned, stepping out of the bathroom, a large towel in his hand. "Or we could start with a massage. Just let me help you off with that wet gown and lie down on the bed over there so we can get started."

Julia whirled around to see that Max was fully dressed once more, although he looked no less dangerous to her peace of mind now than he had when stripped to his shorts.

"Oh, for pity's sake, Max, put a sock in it," she said angrily, grabbing the towel from his outstretched hand before hastily gathering up clean underwear and stomping, back straight and head held high, for the large walk-in closet—that did have a workable lock—to dress for dinner.

Zodiac books her sweet Aunt Millie, she thought meanly, stepping into a pair of lilac silk slacks. She didn't need a book about Leos. What she really needed was a Max Rafferty voodoo doll and a whole fistful of long, sharp pins!

Chapter Eleven

"So tell me, Julia, what were the sleeping arrangements?"

Julia looked across the office at Holly, who was perched on the edge of her desk, her eyes dancing as she stared pointedly at her friend's left ring finger.

"I don't know what you're talking about." Turning her back, Julia quickly removed Max's rings, slipped them into her slacks pocket and transferred Luke's diamond to the correct finger before turning to face her assistant again. "We slept in beds. Or did you think people do it differently in Florida? Really, Holly, you ought to get out more."

Holly rolled her eyes. "I shouldn't have asked. Scorps never give away their secrets. Well, no matter what the sleeping arrangements were, they couldn't have been good. I hate to say this, boss, but you look terrible. Have you told me everything about your father?''

Julia sat behind her desk, resting her elbows on the desktop. "He's fine, Holly, really. As a matter of fact, I'm more worried about my mother right now. She took me into her confidence while I was there and told me that she wants to move back to Allentown.''

Holly came over to perch on the corner of Julia's desk. "And this is a problem? I thought you and your mother were great friends.''

"We are. I'd love it if they moved back, but Mother says it would break Dad's heart to leave Florida. He golfs nearly every day and belongs to some card club at a local social center. The doctor told us his symptoms came from stress. If golfing is stressful, think of how he'd be back here in the dead of winter, shoveling snow. It's a real problem.''

"Not really, sweetheart," Max said from the doorway. "But your parents do have one problem. I think it's called a lack of communication.''

"Max!" Julia stood, glaring across the room at him. "I thought you left for New York as soon as we got back from the airport.''

"I'm just full of surprises these days, aren't I?" he asked, walking around the desk to kiss Julia's pale cheek. "Hello, Holly," he said, grinning at the other woman. "It's good to see you again.''

"It—it's good to see you, too, Mr. Rafferty," Holly stammered, obviously appreciating the effect of the Florida sun on Max's handsome face.

"Call me Max," he corrected absently, once more looking at Julia. "Can we talk?''

Julia barely heard Holly's quick excuses as her assistant hurried from the office. She was too occupied looking at Max, amazed at the quick rush of joy that had welled up in her breast at the sight of him.

After their argument and near passion of the day before, a strained, almost sleepless night spent at opposite ends of the king-size bed, their goodbyes to her parents and a nearly silent plane ride back to Allentown, she had been relieved to arrive home, climb into her own car and bid a quick farewell to Max.

If anyone had told her that barely half an hour later she would be thrilled almost to the point of tears by the mere sight of the man, she would have laughed out loud. See Max again? She wanted nothing more than to forget the man existed. Didn't she?

"What are you doing here, Max? If you still had something to say to me, you had several hours to do so on the plane ride home."

He sat on the edge of her desk and she wildly wondered if she should get rid of the loveseat—after all, nobody seemed to sit on it anymore. "It wasn't the time or the place. I thought we'd talk at your house, but you flew out of there so fast I had no choice but to follow you here. You see, sweetheart, I've been giving this whole thing a lot of thought, and I want you to know what I've decided."

Julia's eyes widened for a fraction of a second and she felt a knot form in the base of her stomach. He was going to give her a divorce. He was giving up the fight, not because he believed he would lose—for Max never thought in terms of defeat—but because he didn't want to fight anymore.

The book said Max's ego was fragile, but she hadn't believed it at the time. Now she wondered. Finding out she had gone behind his back to borrow money from her parents must have hurt his ego even more than she could have imagined. How could Max possibly continue to love someone who had attacked his self-worth and made him feel small, no matter how lofty her motives?

Lofty? Her motives concerning Sutherland had centered more on self-preservation and an unwillingness to be dominated than any notion of righteous independence. She understood that now, even if she hadn't known it then.

She had been too unsure of herself, of her own determination, her own talent, to trust Max within fifty feet of her creation. She had expected him to try to take over her idea and had been ready to sting him the first time he had opened his mouth on the subject. Poor Max. He hadn't had a chance! Why was hindsight always so perfectly twenty-twenty?

She hurried into speech, not wanting to give Max a chance to tell her he was leaving, not wanting to hear her own depressing thoughts and revelations coming out of his mouth. "Look, Max, I'm really busy right now. I mean, one of my jobbers is coming in later, and there's a problem with one of the fabrics I've chosen—just a million little things that need my attention. Can't this wait until later?"

Max shook his head. "No, Julia, it can't. I want to be up-front about this whole business. I've already talked to Luke, and he has agreed to meet me tonight at his place."

"Luke?" Julia had spoken to Luke's service when she had first arrived at the office and was told he was making afternoon rounds at the hospital. "But he's still at the hospital," she said aloud, regretting her words as soon as they were spoken. She should have known Max had been able to talk to Luke. Max could do anything.

"I know." Max smiled. It was an honest smile, showing neither triumph or meanness. "The skateboard kid is going to be fine," he said, picking up a rough sketch of an evening gown and holding it toward the light. "You remember him, the one with the spleen problem. Cute kid."

Of course. Max had gone directly from her house to the hospital. Straight to the source. That was Max. "But I still don't understand. Why do you want to talk to Luke?" she asked warily, reluctantly getting back to the subject at hand.

Max shrugged, the graceful, elegant gesture making Julia long to punch him in the mouth. "It seems only fair," he answered matter-of-factly. "After all, sweetheart, my parents always taught me to be a graceful winner."

Julia felt her mood swing from deep, nebulous despair to a similarly deep but more directed anger. "You're looking for revenge. You're going to tell Luke we slept together!" she exploded, jumping to her feet and a conclusion at the same time. "That's totally beneath you, Max."

"Whoops—I thought you were done. Sorry about that."

Julia looked toward the open door to see Holly in the act of withdrawing herself from the room, a wide grin on her face. She had obviously heard every word of Julia's outburst and drawn her own conclusions.

"Now look what you've done!" Julia accused, whirling to glare at Max.

"Me?" Max asked, pointing at his chest. "What did I do? You're the one who started screaming about our sleeping arrangements. Personally, I don't think it's anybody's business but our own."

"Of course you don't, Max—because nothing happened! You're the last person who would want anyone to know that."

He moved away from the desk. "Right, Julia. And, tell me, who do you know that would believe we slept in the same bed for four nights and yet didn't sleep together? I want to meet him, or her. I think there's still some swampland left in New Jersey I could sell them."

Julia collapsed into her chair. Max was right. Who would believe the truth? Certainly not Holly, just to name one. "What are you going to say to Luke?" she asked again, so weary she felt she could lay her head on the desktop and go to sleep.

Max looked into her eyes as he answered, reminding her of an extremely earnest Boy Scout. "I'm going to tell him that I love you and I'm not going anywhere until you realize that you love me too. I'm here for the duration, Julia, and I have no intention of losing you again."

"Losing me, Max? I don't believe a word of it. Don't you mean you have no intention of losing, period? You say you love me, yet you made no move to get me back in the five years we've been separated."

Max's steady gaze never wavered. "I made a mistake when you left, Julia, standing on my pride like some pompous idiot. But I'm not about to make another one, so you'd better get used to having me around now that I have this second chance. But Luke is in my way, Julia. I like him. I don't want to see him hurt."

"So you set up this meeting tonight to *warn* him?" Julia laughed bitterly. "God, Max, your ego's so big I'm surprised you don't need another body just to carry it around. Tell me, Max, did it ever occur to you that I don't plan to have anything to do with you? That I have seen Max—twice—and I don't want him?"

Max smiled, and Julia's heart plummeted to her toes. "And you tell me, Julia, when we were in Florida, where were you every morning when we woke up? Keep the porch light burning tonight, darling, I may be late."

She watched him leave, unable to speak, remembering that she had awakened every morning locked in Max's arms, their bodies curved together intimately, as if only in slumber could she exhibit her deepest longings.

Max did like Luke Manning. He had seen his work twice, seen two of the young patients he had taken care of and heard two mothers sing the man's praises. Luke was obviously a dedicated physician and a man with a loving, compassionate heart.

He was also Max's rival for Julia's affections which, in a way, made Luke his adversary, and even his enemy.

While Max had little compunction over going for the jugular in business, he was finding it difficult to view the competition between Luke and himself with the same dog-eat-dog ferocity that had made Majestic Enterprises a roaring success.

As he parked his car outside Luke's condo, Max remembered the stricken look in Julia's eyes as he had told her what he planned to do. Julia had always been a sucker for the underdog, as he remembered, and her immediate concern for Luke's welfare had given Max new hope. Obviously, whether she dared to admit it or not, Julia believed that Max was winning the battle to reclaim his wife.

Max knocked on the front door of the brick condo before looking around the suburban neighborhood that seemed to have more than its share of tricycles and station wagons. For a bachelor, Luke Manning didn't seem to mind being surrounded by kids.

"Max," Luke said, opening the door. "I see you didn't have any trouble finding the place. Come on in. I'm on the phone with Julia, but I'll be with you in a minute."

Max stepped inside the small foyer. "Julia? Is she giving you a pep talk or an attack plan?" he asked, heading for the comfortably furnished living room.

Luke laughed aloud as he picked up the receiver, placing one hand over the mouthpiece. "Neither. I think she's hinting at a subtle poison I can slip in your drink."

Max smiled. "That's my girl."

Removing his hand from the mouthpiece Luke spoke into it, saying, "You were right, darling. It's Max. I didn't frisk him, but I believe he's unarmed. Yes, I'll be firm—and serious. Julia, I won't be able to be anything if you won't let me get off the phone. What? All right. Remember, you already told me all that over dinner tonight. I'll call you later. Yes, I promise. Goodbye, darling."

"She hates being relegated to the sidelines," Max commented as Luke, after telling Max he was not on call that evening, walked to the nearby kitchen to get them each a can of beer. "But I congratulate you. How did you convince her to stay away?"

Luke handed Max a can before sitting in the burgundy leather chair that was positioned at a right angle to the couch Max had taken for his own. "It wasn't easy," he admitted, popping open the top of his own can. "And before we begin I think I should tell you Julia explained your sleeping arrangements in Florida and the reasons for them."

Max looked down at the can in his hand. "I'm surprised you didn't bean me with this. I'm not going to lie and tell you I didn't do my best to take advantage of the situation."

Luke sat back, crossing one leg over his other knee. "Why? I would have done the same myself, if I had been in your position. But, as much as I dislike bursting your little bubble, Max, Julia was wearing my ring at dinner tonight."

Max took a long drink from the can, then rested his head against the back of the couch. "Julia," he said, sighing. He sat forward once more. "You know, Luke, it's almost a shame to bring up her name. It puts a wall between us and that saddens me, because I think we could be friends. Good friends. I admire what you do and the reason you do it. You've got quite a heart, Luke, if I'm any judge of character."

Luke held out his can as a sort of salute to Max. "You were Christopher's secret visitor, weren't you, Max? I heard from his mother today. That was a damn nice thing you did for those people. Marcia has taken a new apartment in a better neighborhood and gotten Christopher into a highly recommended day-care center while she finishes her secretarial course. No, Max, I don't have the corner on heart."

Max shrugged, flushing slightly at this praise. "You're the healer, Luke. I only do what I can do." He shook his head, smiling at the other man. "Hey, before this whole thing starts getting sloppy, I think I should tell you why I asked to meet with you tonight. And once I do, I don't think you'll be commissioning any statues in my honor."

Luke went to the kitchen to get two more cans of beer. "I already know why you're here, Max," he called over his shoulder. "Julia made it very clear to me earlier this evening."

"I'll bet she did," Max said, grimacing as he accepted the beer. "She told you she hates me, of course."

"Of course," Luke answered cheerfully, ripping off the second pop top and lifting the can to his lips. "But she doesn't—hate you, that is. I don't think she knows what she feels for you right now."

Max went on the offensive. Leaning forward he declared, "She loves me, Luke. She never stopped loving me."

Luke took another sip of beer. "So you say, Max," he countered quietly. "I suppose she only agreed to marry me out of pity—or desperation?"

The mood in the living room threatened to turn intense. Max was walking a fine line and he knew it. If he overplayed his hand he could end up alienating Luke, which was something he didn't want to do. Julia might not understand that—probably no woman would—but men were different. Men weren't like women. They could be rivals without becoming enemies. They could disagree without losing sight of the fact that, in the end, men had to stick together.

Maybe it was war that did it, or high school football—Max wasn't really sure—but men had always seemed more like team players than women did. All might be fair in love and war, but love was between a man and a woman, and the ultimate war was always waged between the sexes.

If Luke and Julia had gone to bed together, or if Max really believed Julia loved Luke, then it would be different. The law of the jungle would come into play; kill or be killed. But nothing had happened—at least nothing permanent—and Julia wasn't really in love with Luke. She couldn't be in love with him. If she was, she wouldn't have let Max within ten feet of her beloved fiancé.

"Julia didn't make a mistake choosing you, Luke," Max answered at last. "As a matter of fact, if it weren't for me, I'd say you'd make Julia a wonderful husband. You give her lots of space and freedom, which she seems to need, and you don't care the first damn thing about her business other than the fact that it makes her happy.''

"But?" Luke inserted, smiling. "I know there's a 'but' in there somewhere.''

"But," Max said, inclining his head toward Luke as if accommodating the man, "I do exist. I *am* her husband and, although I'll agree with you that I'm one hell of a guy, I'm not about to stand back and give the bride away.'' He set down his half-full can of beer and stood up. "That's the bottom line, and why I came here tonight. I just thought I should warn you, that's all. I'm not going to go away—not without Julia.''

Luke stood as well, holding out his hands to Max. "Fair enough," he said as they shook hands. "I consider myself warned. To tell you the truth, Max, you've been my rival ever since I met Julia a year ago. I had to fight tooth and nail to even get her to go out to dinner with me. She has only been wearing my ring for about two weeks, and for half that time she has been with you. I won't lie and say you don't have me worried, but I'm not going anywhere, either. It's Julia's decision. Now, if that's settled, I think the Philadelphia 76ers are on cable tonight. You like basketball?''

Max stepped back, laughing out loud as he leaned down to pick up his can of beer. "Like it? Hey, your 76ers are playing my Knicks tonight. Would you care to make a small wager on the game?''

As Luke went to the kitchen to make them each a bologna sandwich to "help sop up the beer," Max leaned back against the couch, feeling very good about Luke, their conversation and himself. Yes, he thought smugly, men know how to handle these things.

Chapter Twelve

"**Y**ou never called." Julia spoke the words without preamble as she stood directly inside the door of Luke's private office.

Young patients, parents, nurses and other staff could be heard in the outer office on the other side of the just-closed door, but Julia had barely registered their existence as she had stormed through the throng, her ivory wool cape flying behind her as her high-heeled tan leather boots clicked against the tile floor with each of her determined, long-legged strides.

Luke looked up from the computer printout of blood test results he had been studying. "I'm sorry, darling, but it was very late when Max left. The game ran to double overtime."

"The game," Julia declared coldly, for she recognized that it had come down to either icy disdain or hysterical screaming—she knew she had to do one or the other. "I see. Is that what I am to the two of you, a game? Why didn't you just flip each other for me, or didn't you have a quarter?"

Luke stood and came around the desk to put his hands on Julia's shoulders. "It wasn't like that, darling. Here," he said, guiding her to a chair as she shrugged out of her cape, revealing a cream silk high-necked blouse, a waist-length strand of pearls and a pale camel hair skirt, "sit down and let me explain. I know it looks bad, and I was going to call you first thing this morning, but I had an emergency consultation at the hospital and then, well, I had patients waiting for me here."

Julia shook her head, dismissing his explanation as unnecessary. She wasn't an unreasonable woman; she knew that Luke's work wasn't the sort that could be put on a back burner whenever he had other plans. But that didn't mean she couldn't be hurt by the seeming ease with which he separated his personal and professional life. She, for instance, hadn't been able to concentrate on her work at all the entire morning and Max, although he had maintained contact with his office, had devoted all his time to her, here and in Florida.

"I already spoke to your service, Luke," she explained quickly, trying not to seem petty, "so that isn't the problem. I know it was too late for you to call me last night, because Max didn't come in until after one o'clock. It's just that I was so worried."

She bowed her head. "And maybe a little angry," she added sheepishly, for she was always honest with others, even when she couldn't be honest with herself. She looked up at Luke. "He was *whistling* when he came downstairs this morning, Luke," she hissed through clenched teeth. "Whistling! You don't know how much I wanted to brain the man with a frying pan!"

Luke perched on the end of his desk, reaching down to take Julia's hand. "Didn't he tell you what happened?"

She shook her head, biting her lower lip. "I didn't ask. I wouldn't lower myself. Besides, he wanted to gloat, and I wasn't about to give him that satisfaction."

"Gloat, Julia?" Luke questioned, releasing her hand. "What makes you think Max is entitled to gloat about anything?"

Julia avoided Luke's dark, all-seeing eyes. "No—no reason. No reason in the world. I mean, after all, I'm here, aren't I?"

"It's his ego, isn't it, Julia? The man is so confident, so full of himself and his belief that the whole world can't help but love him."

She stood, walking across the office to look out of the window onto Seventeenth Street and the fairgrounds across the street. "He can't help it," she heard herself say, stung by Luke's words. "Max is just like Wellington. He may be a full-grown man, but he still thinks he's as cute and lovable as a lapdog. He doesn't realize he's steamrolling people. I used to think I envied him, but I don't. You can't envy someone for something that comes so naturally."

She turned to look at Luke, her eyes wide. "My God, Luke, I'm defending the man. Why am I defending the man? Why do I always do that?"

Luke shrugged. "You like him?" he suggested, smiling wryly.

Julia ran a hand through her hair in exasperation. "Like him? *Like* him! I *loathe* him!" She began to pace the length of the room, ticking off the reasons for her feelings on her pink-tipped fingernails. "He's arrogant, egotistical, managing, autocratic, overbearing, totally obtuse to any but his own way of thinking—" She whirled about to confront her fiancé. "They wrote a book about him, you know," she declared feelingly. "Well, at least a chapter."

"They did?" Luke asked, still perched on the desktop.

Julia, caught up in her anger, nodded furiously. "It's a book on the zodiac, actually. Max is a Leo, you understand, born the last week in July. The book described him perfectly. King of the beasts, it calls him—roaring and bellowing, expecting everything to go his way, and sulking if it doesn't. If I hadn't been on the receiving end of most of Max's roars and sulks it might even be funny."

"He sounds terrible, yet I like him very much." Luke walked back around the desk and sat down, still looking at Julia intently. "Didn't this book have anything good to say about poor old Max?"

Julia spread her hands in exasperation. "Oh, sure. It talked about his generosity, his loyalty, his playfulness, his, for want of a better word, lovableness, even his usually sunny disposition, until you cross him, of course. I wouldn't have married him if he hadn't had any redeeming features, would I?''

Luke picked up the test results he had been reading and seemed to be studying them. ''Wouldn't you? I'd imagine the king of beasts would make a fairly exciting lover. I only wish you had something to compare his lovemaking to, but you don't—yet.''

Julia immediately reined in her anger. ''Oh, Luke, I'm sorry,'' she said, going around the desk to put her hand on his shoulder. ''I'm behaving like a child. It's just—it's just that everything is so complicated now. I thought I had my life back together, thought I was beginning a new life, with you, and then Max had to come crashing in, trying to ruin everything.''

Luke reached up to cover her hand with his own. ''He can't ruin anything if it was meant to be in the first place. And it wasn't, Julia. I know that now, and not because Max came to see me last night.''

Julia shivered. ''What—what do you mean?''

''I always knew Max was a tough act to follow, but even I wasn't ready for the full Rafferty treatment.'' Still holding her hand, Luke rose to stand in front of her, looking down into her eyes. ''I mean, darling, that you still love him.''

Julia shook her head vigorously in mute denial. It wasn't true. It couldn't be true. She couldn't love Max. Not again. Yes, she understood him more now than she had five years ago when they had married in the heat of passion, without really taking the time to get to know each other.

Yes, she understood herself more now as well, and had learned that she was a capable individual, able to stand on her own two feet. She didn't need Max to make her feel secure; didn't need his self-assurance to make her believe in her own worth. They were more equal now than they had been, each with their own strengths. But did that mean she was willing to walk back into the lion's den?

"No, Luke," she said at last, her dark eyes pleading with him to understand. "You're wrong. I don't love Max. I like him, I admire him, I may even still envy him a little. I won't deny it. But I don't love him. I don't want to love him. I can't."

Luke smiled, and the sadness of that smile tore at her heart. "You don't hate the man either, Julia, no matter how much you might like to believe otherwise, and you're certainly not indifferent to him. No, we have to face it, and better now than later. You love Max Rafferty."

Julia looked inside herself, searching for answers she had hidden from too long. Long-buried memories flashed in her mind's eye; visions of Max as he had made faces while reading the comics to her, and the way the wind blew his hair onto his forehead as they had walked hand in hand along a deserted beach, talking animatedly, solving all the world's most pressing problems; the way he had looked standing in front of the stove in her Kiss The Cook apron, making his famous Rafferty steaks.

She felt the thrill that had always skittered down her spine as they had entered a party together and all eyes were immediately drawn to them. She felt herself melting as she remembered the touch of his hands, his lips, his body pressed against hers. He had been her world, her entire existence.

Max hadn't just brought her gifts, he was a gift. His love, his loyalty, his reassuring strength—he had openhandedly given her everything she had ever wanted, and she hadn't only loved him, she had adored him. She still adored him, even when she wanted to kill him.

She understood now why she hadn't thrown him out when he had appeared on her doorstep. It didn't matter where Max was, because he was always with her. He had always been with her, from the moment their eyes had met across the classroom five years earlier.

In her heart, she had never really left him, and he had never left her.

Tears welled up in her eyes as she stared into Luke's compassionate face, her fingers working to remove his ring from her finger. "Oh, darling, I'm sorry. I should have known it. I should have seen it sooner. I'm so terribly, terribly sorry. Please forgive me. I'd like to kill Max, but I—I still love him. It must be some sort of curse, don't you think?"

Luke pulled her into his arms, holding her close as she cried into the front of his starched white lab coat. He kissed her, once, a soft, yearning kiss of farewell that tore at her heart. And then he let her go. "I don't blame you for loving Max, Julia. I never had a chance," he told her, pulling out a handkerchief to wipe at her tearstained cheeks.

Julia was devastated. How could she have done such a terrible thing to a man as wonderful as Luke? She felt suddenly angry; angry with herself and angry with

Max. Between them, they had hurt a man whose only mistake had been falling in love with her.

She raised a hand to cup Luke's lean cheek. "I do love you, Luke. I guess I just wasn't in love with you. You deserve better than that, darling," she whispered fervently.

Luke smiled, but it was a sad smile. "Yes," he answered softly. "Yes, I do. But not for a long time. It will take a few years to believe that what we might have had together wasn't the best." He bent to retrieve her cape from the back of the chair. "Now, Julia, if you really do love me, do me one last favor."

"Anything," she promised earnestly, feeling tears begin to sting at her eyes once more.

He looked at her with his intense dark eyes and she experienced a nearly overwhelming need to turn away, unwilling to witness this proud man's pain. "I know this sounds like a cliché from some bad movie, Julia, but please get out of here now, while I'm still strong enough to let you go."

Julia was angry with both herself and Max. But, as it was easier to be angry with Max, she concentrated on that anger for the remainder of the day, as she paced the living room floor, impatiently waiting for him to come home.

Wellington was curled up in front of the fireplace, his big brown eyes watching warily as Julia continued to pace. He had brought her his ball earlier, his usual signal that he wanted to play, but she had only patted his head and turned away. Wellington had been in front of the fireplace ever since, only occasionally heaving a great doggy sigh.

Where could Max have gone? His clothes and suitcase were still in the guest room, even though his car was no longer parked out front. It was eight o'clock, long past her usual dinner hour, but she hadn't eaten—not after opening the refrigerator to see two thick T-bones on the top shelf. It was almost as if Max had known how the day would go and had been planning a celebratory dinner.

Yet Max hadn't come home to cook the steaks, which was probably a good thing, for Julia was sure she would have choked on her very first bite.

"Where is he?" she questioned aloud peevishly, causing Wellington to pick up his head, his ears quivering as if he too was listening for Max's key in the front door. "If he shows up with flowers or a box of candy I may brain him with them!"

Just as she was about to go upstairs to change out of her work clothes, a car door closed out front and Wellington was on his feet heading for the door, his tail wagging furiously.

Julia's pace faltered for a second before speeding up, and she rubbed her hands together as she admonished herself to "be calm, Julia, be calm. This isn't going to be any easier if you yell at him like some fishwife." Just as the key turned in the lock, she scampered for the couch to assume a studied pose of indifference, hastily grabbing a magazine from the coffee table so that it would look as if she had been reading and totally oblivious of the time.

"Hi, hon," Max said cheerfully as he entered the living room, Wellington at his heels. "Sorry I'm late, but I had a meeting with some of my people and lost track of the time."

She closed the magazine with a snap. Would he never cease to surprise her? "You drove to New York for a meeting?"

Shrugging out of his leather coat, he left the room to hang it in the closet before coming back to answer her. "No, that would have taken too long. Jeremy and Paul flew down on the shuttle. They both send their best, by the way. You hungry?" He pushed back the sleeve of his dark blue pin-striped suit to look at his watch. "I turned down Paul's invitation to dinner so I could get back to you. I imagine they're already halfway to Newark airport and a limo ride back into the city."

He was being so casual, not pressing her in any way, yet filling her with tension by the very normalcy of his actions. To an outsider peeking into the living room, it would look as if they were any married couple relaxing at home after work.

Yes, that was what bothered her—he was being too normal. Well, that was one impression she was going to prove wrong right now! She stood, consciously striving to feel she was operating from a position of power.

"That's a pity, Max. Jeremy and Paul could have stayed for dinner and then driven back to New York with you. Your suitcase is all packed and ready to go."

"Oh?" Max looked across the room at her inquiringly. "And what makes you think I'm going to go away that easily, Julia?"

She ran a hand through the top of her hair and it rearranged itself sleekly around her face. "I don't think you're going to go away so easily, Max. I'm not so naive. I think you're going to roar and shout and generally make this a very messy scene. But, in the end, you will go."

"I see," Max said, his usual ruddy complexion deepening by at least two shades. Wellington, who had unearthed his ball once more and stood in front of Max with the thing stuck in his jaws, seemed to sense the tension in the air. Dropping the ball onto Max's left shoe, the dog retired once more to the hearth and, sighing deeply, laid down with his head on his front paws.

"You see?" Julia shook her head. "No, Max, I doubt that you do—not even if I were to draw you a diagram." She walked out from behind the coffee table, her hands wrapped around her waist as she strove to keep her emotions under control. "I gave Luke's ring back to him this afternoon."

Max turned slightly to one side, bent his knees, then stabbed one fist high into the air. *"Yes!"* he shouted, celebrating as if he had just sunk the winning basket with two seconds left in the championship game.

Julia wanted to murder him.

Max sobered immediately, turning to look at his wife. "Is Luke all right?" he asked earnestly, because he knew how he would feel if Julia had chosen the doctor over him. "He wasn't too upset with you?"

"Unlike you, Max, Luke is very civilized," Julia told him quietly, sitting in a nearby chair, her hands gripping the arms tightly, as if to remind her not to stand up again. "As a matter of fact, he was the one who convinced me that I still love you."

Max stood very still, even though he wanted to run and jump and shout his happiness to the world. Julia loved him! Even though he had told himself time and again that she did, he hadn't really allowed himself to believe it until that moment. But something wasn't right. Nobody was kissing anybody. Nobody was falling into anybody's arms, declaring their undying love for anybody.

Then he remembered, and his spirits plummeted to his shoes. She had told him his suitcase was packed. She loved him, but she wanted him gone.

"Julia?" he asked in confusion, taking two steps in her direction, his arms outstretched, ready to gather her close.

"Stop right there, Max," he heard her order imperiously, her expression so bland he knew she must be seething inside, a sleeping volcano on the brink of erupting in smoke and fire.

"I said I love you, Max, but that doesn't mean I want to be married to you again. I may be weak where you're concerned, but that doesn't make me prone to self-destruction."

"Self-destruction!" Max roared in sudden anger, his head beginning to pound. "What the hell is that supposed to mean?"

"It means, Max," she said tightly, "that you don't just love somebody, you have to *possess* them, body, mind, and soul. I can't go back to that. I can't be smothered again."

He had played it all wrong, leaving the house and giving Julia too much time to think, time to build up her defenses. He had known this morning that he was winning, known it from the look on her face and her unwillingness to ask him about his meeting with Luke. But now, even as she admitted to her love, she was sending him away.

She couldn't do that, not now, not when he had finally figured everything out so wonderfully. He wouldn't let her do that.

"Look, Julia," he began, following her into the kitchen, as she had given up her death grip on the arms of the chair and was trying to make her escape, "I think you're overreacting. You always did—"

"Oh, *really?*" She whirled about to face him, fire in her eyes. "And just what is *that* supposed to mean, Max?"

He grabbed her shoulders, unwilling to have this argument on the run, with Julia skipping from room to room while he scampered along behind her like some supplicant begging for an audience. "It means, Julia, that all this business about me dominating you is nothing but a bunch of hogwash. Nobody could dominate you, Julia, if they had an army of giants behind him! You just couldn't take it when you found out that it's a two-way street and *you* couldn't dominate me!"

Julia's head snapped back. "That's *not* true! Dominate you? Don't make me laugh. Besides, the handsome, wonderful King Max was always too busy issuing orders to his lowly peasants—when he wasn't smiling down on them graciously and handing them gifts—to stand still long enough to be dominated."

Max smiled, not knowing he was nearly blinding her with the brilliant sunlight of his sudden return to good humor. "Handsome and wonderful, huh?" he asked, diverted to her backhanded compliment. "I like the king thing too, come to think of it. Actually, Julia, I can't imagine why you ever left, if I was that great. Let's kiss and make up. You remember how much we always liked that."

"Ohhh!" Julia all but shrieked, pulling free of his arms. "I must be out of my mind! Luke and that silly book were both right—you have the largest ego in captivity!"

Max's smile froze in place and his hands dropped from Julia's shoulders. He couldn't believe what he had just heard. He didn't care about the book— probably the book Holly had asked him to give to Julia—but he did care about the doctor's opinion of him. "Luke said that?"

"He didn't mean it." Julia collapsed into a nearby chair. "Luke is a very intelligent, perceptive man. He only said it so I would defend you which, God help me, I did. You may have faults, Max, but for some ridiculous reason I can't stand to hear anyone else point them out. That's my job."

"Your job, huh?" Max sat down across the table from her, cupping his chin in his hands. "Well, I'll say one thing, you do it very well," he said slowly, inclining his head in her direction.

Julia seemed confused. "Th-thank you," she said, frowning.

Max sensed that she was weakening, but he knew he wasn't going to be happy with her surrender. They didn't need to reconcile. They needed a whole new beginning, and the strongest foundations were built on honesty. He loved this woman more than life itself, and if he had to crawl over the broken glass of his own ego to get her back, he'd do it.

Max decided to take one last shot, rolling for all the marbles. "I can't blame you for criticizing me. As a matter of fact, sweetheart, there have been times when I believe you've raised criticism of me to an art form. Tell me, Julia, would it help if I told you I've learned my lesson?"

"Meaning," Julia asked, looking across the table at him, her dark eyes unreadable.

"Meaning, dear wife, that I know now that you only kept your maiden name for business as your way of showing me that I was to butt out of that part of your life. The same thing goes for Sutherland itself, which is why you borrowed the seed money from Jim rather than come to me. Am I right so far?"

"Congratulations, Max," Julia said, nodding. "And to think it only took you five years to figure it out."

Max, sensing that he had the advantage now, went to Julia and pulled her to her feet. "I'm not usually so slow, sweetheart, but I had to break through my pride first in order to see what was staring me in the face. Besides, I rather like being in charge."

Julia allowed him to pull her into his arms. "Now *there's* a news bulletin."

"You always did have a smart mouth, darling, but go ahead, I can take it." He rested his chin on her head, feeling desire rising inside him but forcing himself to take it slow. "I can take anything, as long as I have you by my side. I know you don't believe this, but I'm not always as sure of myself as I would like people to believe. You make me feel powerful—just in the way you look at me. It's as if you believe I can do anything and yet, if I should fail, you'd be there for me anyway. I've missed that, sweetheart, and, well, I'm not sure I can live the rest of my life without it."

"Oh, Max, thank you," Julia said on a sigh as she allowed him to draw her even closer into his embrace. "You can't know how much *I've* needed to hear that you need me."

Max closed his eyes, silently glorying in the knowledge that the worst was over. They were going to be all right. Later, much later, he'd tell her about his new, wonderful idea.

"Yes, well, as long as I'm being honest—and I'm only telling you this because I love you—I might as well admit that I also seem to have a small problem with admitting that I'm wrong. It was easier to blame you for our breakup. It still would be easier, as a matter of fact. You wouldn't want to apologize or anything, would you? Just to ease my stubborn, overblown ego?"

Julia lifted her head to smile up into his face, her lovely dark eyes awash in tears. "No, I don't think I would," she said, slipping her arms around his neck.

"But there may be a way we both can win. I must be crazy for asking this, but would a kiss do as well?"

Max grinned wickedly, triumph in his eyes, as his mouth descended to claim hers.

Epilogue

Max had done a lot of difficult things in his life, but leaving Julia that night and returning to New York ranked very near the top of the list. Much as Julia had wanted to thank him for the thought and then change his mind and lead him upstairs to her bed, Max knew this was one thing he had to do.

They had married in haste, eloping without telling Julia's parents and saying their vows in front of a yawning justice of the peace. Maybe it wouldn't have made any difference in the outcome of their five-month marriage, but Max liked to believe that having a real wedding, exchanging their vows in front of a minister with family and a few friends as witnesses would make their marriage stronger.

Of course, as with everything Max did, the wedding ceremony that took place three weeks later was very large, with several hundred of Max's closest friends tactfully spreading themselves out on both sides of the aisle to make up for Julia's small family and more moderate number of guests.

Jim Sutherland, his smiling face aglow with health, escorted his daughter down the aisle of the small church in Cape May, New Jersey, the site of Max and Julia's first, abbreviated honeymoon. Jim had every reason to smile, now that he and Margaret were installed in Julia's lovely house on Hamilton Street and Jim had taken over the local management of Sutherland.

Julia had been ecstatic when Max had proposed his plan to her, as it had answered all their problems, leaving her free to design her collection from their Manhattan apartment. She hadn't even told him that he was trying to run her life again, because she knew he wasn't. Max was just being his usual, brilliant, take-charge self.

Jim and Margaret, at Max's prompting, had admitted to each other their unhappiness with the laid-back, retired life, and Jim's doctor had heartily endorsed his return to work. Only back in Allentown for ten days, Margaret had already bought a new winter coat, rejoined her bridge club and signed up to volunteer at Luke's children's clinic.

Luke Manning had not dropped out of Julia's life entirely, even agreeing to come to the wedding, although in the end a last-minute emergency kept him from the ceremony. Julia and Max were genuinely sorry he couldn't be there.

Julia was regally yet touchably beautiful as she came down the aisle on her father's arm, her tea-length gown of palest peach lace one of her own creations. Her chin high, she kept her steady gaze concentrated on her groom, who stood to one side of the aisle, looking very handsome and endearingly nervous.

Max took her hand as she approached and, together, they stood before the minister to give their responses in the marriage ceremony.

Everything went very well for the first few minutes, with Margaret and Holly, Julia's single attendant, sniffling delicately into their handkerchiefs, until the minister instructed Max to "repeat your vows after me."

The justice of the peace may have mumbled the words, or Julia may have been too nervous that first time to take too much notice of them, but things were different now. She was listening to every word, her eyes downcast as she enjoyed the sight of Max's hand clasping hers as he prepared to slip the wide gold band on her finger.

"Place the ring on her finger, please, and say after me," the minister said solemnly, "I, Maximillian Leo Rafferty—"

Julia's eyes widened in sudden surprise and she smiled up at her clearly amused bridegroom, the two of them oblivious to anyone else in the church.

"Leo!" she exclaimed in delight as Max winked and lovingly squeezed her hand. "Oh, darling, I should have known!"

MORE ABOUT
THE LEO MAN

by Lydia Lee

If you're interested in living like royalty, having a mate who is generous, noble and warmhearted, then look no further than the King of the Zodiac: Leo, the lion! When it comes to romancing, wining, dining and picking up the check, this is your man. Actually, you can't say enough wonderful things about him, and if you're interested in catching his eye, you'd better know from the start, he thrives on attention and flattery. Mind you, don't go overboard and fawn all over His Highness; that wouldn't do at all. *His Highness?* Believe me, if you've ever been courted by a Leo male, you'll know what I mean.

To begin with, there's usually something regal about his bearing, almost as if he *were* a king. (Remember how Napoleon crowned himself?) The man also has a way of attracting subjects; they sort of orbit around him like little satellites. Give this lion an audience and he's in his element. Of course, underneath all that flash, he's really a pussycat—and if you want to hear him purr loud and clear, *you* be his audience. On the other hand, if you want to know how ferocious his roar really is, just try flirting with another man!

Ah, you may be quick to point out, *he* flirts with other women! Still, let's not convict him too hastily. To begin with, he'll assure you he was only looking, and chances are that will be the truth. These men love to window shop, so you'd best not reproach him or you'll run the risk of truly hurting his feelings. Yes, hurting his feelings, because, for all his showmanship and grand gestures, he secretly fears failure and rejection. It can instantly crush that magnificent spirit in him, and there isn't a more miserable sight to see than a dejected lion. Remember the Cowardly Lion in *The Wizard of Oz?* Well, in part, your Leo man shares some of those traits. He really does fear that he doesn't have what it takes to succeed in life or to get that promotion or to win his lady love. That's why, every now and then, he has to roar so loudly. But when push comes to shove, his courage takes over. Then he discovers he really can do whatever he sets out to do and that he *is* a tower of strength and courage. Someday he'll even realize he is a king and not just a pretender.

There's one other thing you'd better know about your Sun-ruled Leo: his need for love runs a neck-and-neck race with his need for success and for being the center of attention. However, without love and the right woman in his life, all the trophies and applause in the world will pale next to that shining, illusive thing called love. Just knowing this about that devastatingly attractive bachelor you met by the coffee urn at work will put you leagues ahead of the other women who'll undoubtedly be stalking him. *Stalking* is the right word, too, because there's simply something about him that brings out a woman's deepest passions and most outrageous fantasies. Think Robert Redford. And remember, be the Leo man's audience.

This is certainly not to say that he wants a mindless woman—far from it. But the thought of some shrew trying to dethrone him sets the lion into a panic. On the other hand, you—as his loving partner and pro- verbial power behind the throne—will elicit such de- votion, passion and true love, that being his audience will be a small price to pay. He'll be king of his castle, and as his queen, you can be assured of the kind of life many women only dream of or read about in ro- mance novels. But this man will be very real and, true to his fire sign, *very passionate,* as those of you who share his bed and castle know.

If he sounds like your royal cup of tea, the line forms to your left. Possibly it's at the stage door of your local theater. Leos are considered by some as- trologers to be the most creative sign of the Zodiac, so it's natural to find them trodding the boards and spouting Shakespeare. They also make wonderful teachers and get along beautifully with children. In short, look for your Leo in any profession that gives him access to the public and allows him to fulfil his creative abilities.

*   *   *   *   *

Famous Leo Men

Mick Jagger
Cecil B. DeMille
Robert Mitchum
George Bernard Shaw
Napoleon Bonaparte

WRITTEN IN THE STARS

Love's in Sight!
THROUGH MY EYES
by Helen R. Myers

Dr. Benedict Collier was the perfect
Virgo—poised, confident, always in
control... until an accident left him
temporarily blinded. But nurse Jessica
Holden wasn't about to let Ben languish in
his hospital bed. This was her chance to
make Ben open his eyes to the *love* he'd
resisted for years!

THROUGH MY EYES
by Helen R. Myers... coming from
Silhouette Romance this September.
It's WRITTEN IN THE STARS!

Available in September at your favorite retail outlet, or order your copy now by sending your
name, address, zip code or postal code, along with a check or money order for $2.59 (please
do not send cash), plus 75¢ postage and handling ($1.00 in Canada). payable to Silhouette
Reader Service to:

In the U.S.
3010 Walden Avenue
P.O. Box 1396
Buffalo, NY 14269-1396

In Canada
P.O. Box 609
Fort Erie, Ontario
L2A 5X3

Please specify book title with your order
Canadian residents add applicable federal and provincial taxes

SEPTSTAR-RR

Silhouette Romance®

Bestselling author NORA ROBERTS captures all the romance, adventure, passion and excitement of Silhouette in a special miniseries.

THE CALHOUN WOMEN

Four charming, beautiful and fiercely independent sisters set out on a search for a missing family heirloom—an emerald necklace—and each finds something even more precious... passionate romance.

Look for THE CALHOUN WOMEN miniseries starting in June.

COURTING CATHERINE
in Silhouette Romance #801 (June/$2.50)

A MAN FOR AMANDA
in Silhouette Desire #649 (July/$2.75)

FOR THE LOVE OF LILAH
in Silhouette Special Edition #685 (August/$3.25)

SUZANNA'S SURRENDER
in Silhouette Intimate Moments #397 (September/$3.29)

Available at your favorite retail outlet, or order any missed titles by sending your name, address, zip code or postal code, along with a check or money order (please do not send cash) for the price shown above, plus 75¢ postage and handling ($1.00 in Canada), payable to Silhouette Reader Service to:

In the U.S.
3010 Walden Avenue
P.O. Box 1396
Buffalo, NY 14269-1396

In Canada
P.O. Box 609
Fort Erie, Ontario
L2A 5X3

Please specify book title(s) with your order.
Canadian residents add applicable federal and provincial taxes.

CALWOM-2R

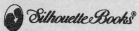 Silhouette Books®

Silhouette Romance®

LONG, TALL TEXANS

EVAN
Diana Palmer

Diana Palmer's bestselling LONG, TALL TEXANS series continues with EVAN....

Anna Cochran is nineteen, blond and beautiful—and she wants Evan Tremayne. Her avid pursuit of the stubborn, powerfully built rancher had been a source of amusement in Jacobsville, Texas, for years. But no more. Because Evan Tremayne is about to turn the tables...and pursue her!

Don't miss EVAN by Diana Palmer, the eighth book in her LONG, TALL TEXANS series. Coming in September...only from Silhouette Romance.

SRLTT

SILHOUETTE·INTIMATE·MOMENTS®

IT'S TIME TO MEET
THE MARSHALLS!

In 1986, bestselling author Kristin James wrote A VERY SPECIAL FAVOR for the Silhouette Intimate Moments line. Hero Adam Marshall quickly became a reader favorite, and ever since then, readers have been asking for the stories of his two brothers, Tag and James. At last your prayers have been answered!

In August, look for THE LETTER OF THE LAW (IM #393), James Marshall's story. If you missed youngest brother Tag's story, SALT OF THE EARTH (IM #385), you can order it by following the directions below. And, as our very special favor to you, we'll be reprinting A VERY SPECIAL FAVOR this September. Look for it in special displays wherever you buy books.

Available now at your favorite retail outlet, or order your copy by sending your name, address, zip or postal code, along with a check or money order for $3.25 (please do not send cash), plus 75¢ postage and handling ($1.00 in Canada), payable to Silhouette Reader Service to:

In the U.S.
3010 Walden Ave.
P.O. Box 1396
Buffalo, NY 14269-1396

In Canada
P.O. Box 609
Fort Erie, Ontario
L2A 5X3

Please specify book title with your order.
Canadian residents add applicable federal and provincial taxes.

MARSH-3

Silhouette Books®

FOUR UNIQUE SERIES
FOR EVERY WOMAN YOU ARE...

Silhouette Romance®

Tender, delightful, provocative—stories that capture the laughter, the tears, the *joy* of falling in love. Pure romance...straight from the heart!

SILHOUETTE *Desire*®

Go wild with Desire! Passionate, emotional, sensuous stories of fiery romance. With heroines you'll like and heroes you'll *love*, Silhouette Desire never fails to deliver.

Silhouette Special Edition®

Stories of love and life, these powerful novels are tales that you can identify with—romances with "something special" added in! Silhouette Special Edition is entertainment for the heart.

SILHOUETTE·INTIMATE·MOMENTS®

Enter a world where passions run hot and excitement is the rule. Dramatic, larger-than-life and always compelling—Silhouette Intimate Moments will never let you down.

SGENERIC